THE DECADENT GIFT

AN AFTER DARK NOVEL

LAUREN BLAKELY

LITTLE DOG PRESS

ALSO BY LAUREN BLAKELY

Big Rock Series

Big Rock

Mister O

Well Hung

Full Package

Joy Ride

Hard Wood

The Gift Series

The Engagement Gift

The Virgin Gift

The Decadent Gift

The Heartbreakers Series

Once Upon a Real Good Time

Once Upon a Sure Thing

Once Upon a Wild Fling

Boyfriend Material

Asking For a Friend

Sex and Other Shiny Objects

One Night Stand-In

Lucky In Love Series

Best Laid Plans

The Feel Good Factor

Nobody Does It Better

Unzipped

Always Satisfied Series

Satisfaction Guaranteed

Instant Gratification

Overnight Service

Never Have I Ever

Special Delivery

The Sexy Suit Series

Lucky Suit

Birthday Suit

From Paris With Love

Wanderlust

Part-Time Lover

One Love Series

The Sexy One

The Only One

The Hot One

The Knocked Up Plan

Come As You Are

Sports Romance

Most Valuable Playboy

Most Likely to Score

Standalones

Stud Finder

The V Card

The Real Deal

Unbreak My Heart

The Break-Up Album

21 Stolen Kisses

Out of Bounds

The Caught Up in Love Series:

The Swoony New Reboot of the Contemporary Romance Series

The Pretending Plot (previously called *Pretending He's Mine*)

The Dating Proposal

The Second Chance Plan (previously called *Caught Up In Us*)

The Private Rehearsal (previously called *Playing With Her Heart*)

Stars In Their Eyes Duet

My Charming Rival

My Sexy Rival

The No Regrets Series

The Start of Us

The Thrill of It

Every Second With You

The Seductive Nights Series

First Night (Julia and Clay, prequel novella)

Night After Night (Julia and Clay, book one)

After This Night (Julia and Clay, book two)

One More Night (Julia and Clay, book three)

A Wildly Seductive Night (Julia and Clay novella, book 3.5)

The Joy Delivered Duet

Nights With Him (A standalone novel about Michelle and Jack)

Forbidden Nights (A standalone novel about Nate and Casey)

The Sinful Nights Series

Sweet Sinful Nights

Sinful Desire

Sinful Longing

Sinful Love

The Fighting Fire Series

Burn For Me (Smith and Jamie)

Melt for Him (Megan and Becker)

Consumed By You (Travis and Cara)

The Jewel Series

A two-book sexy contemporary romance series

The Sapphire Affair

The Sapphire Heist

ABOUT

The rules of the game were simple.

One weekend.

We play our roles. Actually, we play *lots* of roles.

I get the info I need for a secret work project.

We go back to how we were.

That's what I proposed to handsome, clever, commanding Jake.

That's what he said yes to—this decadent gift of a weekend that would get me out of debt.

But that's not what happened when our nights together in Vegas ended . . .

THE DECADENT GIFT

By Lauren Blakely

Want to be the first to learn of sales, new releases, preorders and special freebies? Sign up for my VIP mailing list here!

1

KATE

I had a dirty little secret.

Those were the best kind.

And the worst too.

Because sometimes secrets could torment you.

Like at night when you were alone.

Or during the day when your mind wandered to what-ifs. I had so many what-ifs running through my head.

As I weaved my way through the casino, checking out the crowds, scanning the couples tangled up in each other, the women sliding close to their men, the men dropping kisses on their cheeks, the latest possibility pulsed inside me.

Just a regular day in Las Vegas.

Then, I walked past the roulette tables, headed toward the restaurant where I was meeting my friends, and I spotted a new boutique.

New to The Luxe Hotel, that was.

Ava's, a well-known lingerie shop, had moved last

month from the Bellagio to here, peddling an eye-catching assortment of lace and satin that beckoned shoppers through the windows.

But that wasn't what first caught my eye.

It was a sign next to the display, where a lightbox flashed in lush pink: *Explore Your Fantasies.*

Might as well be my mantra.

It was what I'd encouraged my girlfriends to do when they'd come to me for advice.

I preached it like a religion.

"Are you reading my mind, Ava?" I whispered.

Maybe so, because I was a card-carrying believer in delving into your dirty dreams.

Trouble was, I'd yet to explore all of mine.

Not the way I wanted to.

Not the way I craved. I'd never met the kind of man who'd take that journey with me. But still, the possibilities were powerful and alluring, flitting through my mind like will-o'-the-wisps just out of reach.

I peered at the white door to the shop, open, inviting.

Hard to resist.

Music pulsed low, drifting faintly out of the shop into the cavernous hallway, some Corinne Bailey Rae number that suggested nudity was on the menu.

Well, it *was* a lingerie shop. The kind of lingerie meant to be taken off.

Meant for exploring fantasies.

Would this store hold the key to unlock mine?

I shivered as I pictured scenarios of entangled bodies, desires, and longing.

Of hot, naughty nights.

And words, so many filthy words spilling from lips.

I stepped into the store, my heels sinking into the plush pink carpet.

Ava's was no clandestine sex dungeon, but when I spotted a display in the far corner of the store, I grinned, whispering, "That's what I'm talking about."

Elegant French maid costumes. Insanely sexy stewardess uniforms. Schoolgirl skirts that left little to the imagination.

No, that wasn't my kink. I wasn't a costume-play girl. More power to the ones who were, but that didn't do it for me . . . except in how they suggested scenes, just a few in the endless array of scenarios I could imagine.

The games. The role-play. The infinite possibilities.

If a couple came in to buy a schoolgirl costume, what sort of script would they follow that night?

What might unfold between a flight attendant and a first-class passenger on a transatlantic flight?

What if, what if, oh yes, *what if.*

A slight shiver ran through me.

"Anything catch your eye?"

The sultry, smoky voice drew me back from speculation to reality. I turned to a willowy blonde behind the counter.

"All of it," I said with a smile, raising an eyebrow at the items in the corner.

She smiled back. "Glad to hear you like what we have."

But I wasn't so interested in *my* likes. Since I'd never

met a question that I wouldn't ask, I voiced the one foremost in my mind. "Are they selling well?"

Translation: are there role-playing games transpiring all around us right now, this minute?

"Indeed." Her satisfied grin hinted that she had a naughty secret, and I wondered briefly what it might be. Maybe she was buying up the naughty nurse garb. "We added them last week. They're a big part of our store's mission." Her gaze drifted to the displays. "Is there anything particular you're looking for in that arena?"

I could have answered that question in many ways. The most honest would have been *I'm merely interested in the games people play.*

But before I could fashion any sort of reply, my phone trilled from the pocket of my purse—my boss's ringtone.

I smiled apologetically, patting my purse. "Another time," I told the blonde.

She nodded. "We'll be here when you're ready."

Something about that stuck with me. *When you're ready.* I liked how it implied the opportunity would inevitably come. It wouldn't pass me by.

Right now, though, I had to be ready for a call with Trish Valentine.

I always had to be ready for my twenty-four-seven boss. But that suited me just fine—work and the paychecks that came with it were what I needed most in my life.

Not fantasies. Not mine, and not anyone else's.

I shucked off those distractions as I stepped out of the store and into the wide hallway.

"Hi, boss lady," I said into the phone, keeping it as upbeat as she liked.

Trish laughed, a familiar throaty sound. "Haven't I told you that Queen of the Night will do? That's all I require."

It was an apt title, given some of our more risqué clients. "Queen of the Night you are, and I am but your humble servant."

I could sense the eye roll from across the city. "Please, you're my right-hand gal, Kate. I can't do this without you." Trish's assurances were genuine, her tone as kind as she was. Despite the you're-on-call treatment, the woman was warm and caring.

"Which is why I'm calling," she went on. "I'm on my way to an appointment, but we just landed a new client, and I want you to take the lead. I'll give you the details tomorrow. It will be amazing, but we need to move quickly for them. They're rolling out new products right away."

My ears perked. Everything perked. Trish had been hinting at some new work for her marketing firm, where I was a vice president. New work for us meant potential bonus money for me. And I needed every extra shade of green. *Badly.* "This is the client you've been angling for?"

"Yes indeed. It's a woman-centric company. The messaging needs to be spot-on for females who love this city. I need you to be my woman on the ground. You know Vegas, you know young women, and you know what makes them tick. Be thinking about girls' night out marketing."

Ah, so girls' nights out—that was what the client did. Perhaps arranged them? Organized bachelorette parties? "What kind of girls' night out?"

"The *extra fun* kind," she said, teasing. "I'll tell you more in the morning. Must go. My driver is here."

Before she hung up, I heard her purr, "Hello, Daniel."

Intrigued, I filed that—*hello, Daniel*—away. Was she having a fling with her driver?

But now wasn't the time to linger on my boss's preferences—there was *never* a time to do that—so I turned my mind to the scant breadcrumb trail of information she'd tossed out.

Be thinking about girls' night out marketing.

That was a little broad, and secretive too. But then, so was my job, marketing the after-hours world I inhabited here in Sin City. Most of our clients preferred we operated under the radar, marketing them in subtle, nuanced ways.

I rounded the bend, heading for the restaurant.

A dinner out with my best friends could only help prepare me for this secretive meeting tomorrow to talk about girls' night marketing.

The *extra fun* kind.

2

KATE

Through the edamame appetizer, miso soup, and seaweed salad, I pondered this city.

What it offered in nights out.

Vegas was a pleasure palace, and you could have any extravagance you desired for the right amount of money. Everything had a price tag.

It was the kind of city where you could buy, barter, win, or lose anything.

Bets were only the beginning.

You could arrange for nights out, nights in, nights with men, nights with women, and nights with a mix. Like in a cupcake box, you could pick your flavor, make your sampler, and take it home.

Devour it.

Vegas was a hamlet for freedom of the nighttime variety. The city encouraged exploration of your fantasies because Vegas let you shed your inhibitions after dark.

In a city where anything went, nothing stayed forbidden. It was a city of *why not.*

That was what I would lean on tomorrow during the meeting.

Those notions.

Tonight, though, was for research.

As Lily, Nina, and I moved on to our rainbow rolls, my gaze drifted to a clutch of women in full bachelorette-party garb sauntering toward the sushi joint's bar.

The bride wore a tiara and a white sash with THE ALMOST MRS. written in black Sharpie across it, while the bridesmaids hyped themselves as THE BRIDE SQUAD. They made a beeline for the bartender, squealing their orders—one cosmo, one lemon drop, a margarita, and a vodka tonic. The woman I pegged as the maid of honor ordered a round of tequila shots.

Perhaps I could learn something useful as prep for Trish's last-minute assignment. What made a great girls' night out?

Sometimes you focused on finding sex, and sometimes you celebrated friendships—different strokes for different women folk.

Time to go fishing and see what I might catch.

I leaned in closer to my friends, dropping my voice. "Let's play a game," I suggested. "It'll help me with my meeting tomorrow. We'll even have stakes. A gentlewoman's bet, if you will."

"Ooh. You're letting us into your secret work world. This ought to be good. What's the meeting about?" Lily asked as she reached for a roll with her chopsticks. She loved to give me a hard time about my boss's don't-ask-don't-tell vibe.

"I don't have all the details yet. But Trish called an hour ago to tell me we landed a new client who wants to focus on girls' night out marketing, and we don't have much time to get it going, so I want to be in tip-top shape with my . . . *talking points*," I said, finishing the sentence in the same tone my boss used when she spoke to her driver.

A sexy little purr.

Nina arched a brow above the frame of her red glasses. "Only you could make the phrase *talking points* sound deliciously sensual."

I grinned, then blew on my burgundy fingernails. "That's my job, girls. Make everything sound enticing."

"You are the best at leading the denizens of this city to the enchanted forest of naughty," Lily added.

I winked at her. "Because everyone wants to be led. I'm a tour guide into the magical land of dirty fairy tales." That was an apt description of the type of marketing work I handled. Plenty of my clients wanted the typical splash and fanfare of a marketing campaign, like the casinos, celebrity chef pop-up restaurants, and new designer boutiques we handled. But others, such as the occasional gentleman's club or high-stakes players' games, required a more unconventional approach to reach the right clientele.

"What's the game, then? And what are the rules and the stakes?" Lily asked as she dipped her roll in soy sauce.

I tipped my forehead in the direction of the bride squad. "The game is this—what are they up to tonight?"

"The bride and her posse?" Nina asked.

"Yes. Let's make our best guesses as to the agenda for their Thursday night," I said in a low voice. "The rules are simple. Whoever makes the best case, wins."

"You and your love of bets," Nina said with a smile and a shake of her head.

"Me and my bets," I echoed.

"What are the stakes?" Nina asked, a skeptical note in her voice. "Better not be a free latte, because I already have one of those coming tomorrow thanks to my coffee-shop loyalty card." She preened. "I got my tenth punch today. It's okay to be jealous."

I laughed at the pun she might not have intended. "You're all about getting cards punched lately, aren't you?" I teased, unable to resist tweaking my good friend, who shed her virginity mere months ago with her next-door neighbor.

She'd chosen well. Adam was now her fiancé.

Nina shot me an *oh no you didn't* look. "You really went there?"

"She really went there," Lily added as she laughed.

Nina rolled her eyes. "Fine, fine. Yes, after I punched my V-card, I set to work on my coffee-shop bucket list," she said in a singsong voice. "I'm working through latte drinks now instead of sex positions. Anyway, back to your game, dirty fairy godmother."

I set a hand on my chest. "*C'est moi.*" I exhaled, returning to the rules. "For stakes—how about winner chooses dessert for us to share?"

"Dessert is a vital item on a girls' night out menu," Lily said, and Nina nodded her agreement.

I set down my chopsticks, nodded to the bride pack, then imitated the *Jeopardy!* countdown clock. "For choice of dessert, Alex, this is what the crew will be doing tonight . . ."

Nina whipped her gaze around, studying the ladies, a serious look in her brown eyes.

Lily stared too, her brow furrowing as she seemed to take mental notes on the women, her reporter's radar surely firing. "What is a bar crawl, a limo ride, and a nighttime pool party?" she declared.

Interesting picks. But why had she chosen those? The *why* was critical in any marketing pursuit. "And your reasoning?"

"One of the ladies is wearing a bikini," Lily said, stating the facts. "But the series of drinks tells me it's going to be a long night at the bar, and long nights at the bar usually involve limos. And limos are fun with friends."

"True that." I pointed to Nina. "Your turn."

"I'm rolling the dice in a different direction. Since they're giving off a man-candy vibe, I say, what is Magic Mike Live, Chippendales, and a round of slots along the way? Probably at the Aladdin slot machine."

I raised my brow at Nina's addendum. "That's oddly specific." I wiggled my fingers, urging her to serve it up. "I need more detail on the Aladdin bit."

"Have you seen Jafar on the slot machine by the roulette table? He's hotter than a desert day," Nina said, a naughty glint in her brown eyes.

Picturing the villain on the machine, I hummed my appreciation—for her answer, and the slot machine hottie. "Jafar doesn't always get his due. Of all the villains, he's probably the most bangable," I admitted.

"Live-action Jafar, that is," Lily put in, licking her lips.

"Yes," I said, laughing as I pictured the recent flick. "I'm definitely talking about live-action Jafar. I can resist the cartoon one easily. But Mr. Tall, Dark, Handsome, and Decidedly Nefarious is hard to look away from."

"Let's raise a glass to all the hot villains," Nina said, then turned the game back to me. "Your turn, Kate. What do you imagine they're up to?"

I drew a deep inhalation, putting on my observation hat. The one I *loved* wearing. Because this was my world —what-ifs and scenarios.

I rolled through some in my mind. Would they go for a traditional bachelorette party–style night, with bawdy girl-centric activities? Perhaps a night of dancing and clubbing? Or something a little wilder?

As I hunted for clues, the bride squeezed the maid of honor's shoulder, then draped an arm around her. She shot her a sympathetic smile.

Interesting.

Typically, the bride squad bestowed all its attention on the bride. But this was a reversal, and it was all the info I needed.

"What is hot sex with a stranger?"

Lily blinked.

Nina emitted a "*Whoa.*"

I owned my answer, and not simply because stranger sex was one of the best kinds. "The bride wants to find a hot guy for her maid of honor. She wants to get her friend laid tonight. I can sense it. That's what their body language is telling me."

Lily narrowed her eyes at the bride and maid of honor, and Nina did the same, both watching intently. A few seconds later, they snapped their gazes back to me. "Damn. You are good," Lily said. "I'm getting that vibe too."

"Yeah, I'm just going to say it now. There are no two ways about it—I'm voting for you as the winner," Nina said. "And you better pick a good dessert."

Lily raised a hand in question. "I like your answer. But would the bride stop at just the maid of honor? Why doesn't she arrange for hot sex for all the single members of the bridal party?"

Nina waggled her chopsticks, reaching for a roll. "If she's a magnanimous bride, she should make sure all her available ladies-in-waiting are taken care of," she added, pointing her eel roll at me. "And I'm happy to find a hot guy for you if that's what you're getting at . . ." she trailed off, like she wanted me to jump on the tantalizing offer.

I shook my head. I wasn't truly tempted. "I'm not angling for either of you to supply me with a man."

I didn't have time for relationships or their attendant complications, not when I had a kick-ass job demanding more than 100 percent of me.

A job that paid well, I might add.

Being well paid was a critical necessity, considering the way my ex had left.

Lily wiggled her eyebrows at me. "But someday we can set you up?"

"You have such a matchmaker in you. But you know the answer to that. I'm not in the market for accouterments."

Nina laughed. "Is that what we call sex? An accouterment?"

I smiled, patting my bargain-basement Coach purse. "Like a fabulous handbag or a great new pair of shoes."

"So, sex is an accessory," Lily said, deadpan.

"It dresses up any night, any weekend, any event," I said, stopping to take a drink of my wine. "Or so I hear. It's been a while."

Nina shot me a sympathetic look. "You're almost there though?" She knew I'd been man-free for the last year as I worked to claw myself out of the pile of debt my ex left behind in my name.

Such a lovely parting gift.

I held up my hand, crossing my fingers. "Just a few more thousand, and I'll be done."

Lily patted my forearm. "You've done an amazing job."

I shrugged. "Didn't have any other choice, but I'm glad the end is in sight."

That was why I dove into every work challenge Trish tossed my way. The better we did, the more I earned, the closer I came to moving all the way on from the grip of the past and the specter of my own mistake in getting involved with Damon.

I should have seen it coming.

Should have studied Damon a little better, observed him more closely.

Maybe if I'd been more cautious, I wouldn't have wound up saddled with his money problems while he was off gallivanting in the Caribbean. Or wherever it was that asshole exes went to gallivant.

"And that's why this meeting tomorrow is important. This campaign might give me just enough to be done with Damon's baggage. Your ideas for the bachelorette party's plans might be useful when it comes to market research tomorrow. So thank you for helping," I added.

"I'm glad you have some fodder for your girls' night out meeting," Nina said, then checked the time on her phone. "Especially since ours is about to turn into a mixed night out."

"And on that note, I need to pop into the ladies'," I said.

I grabbed my purse and excused myself for the restroom.

Along the way, my phone buzzed with a text. Stopping in the hallway, I slid my thumb across the screen, a sliver of a smile tugging at my lips when I saw the name of the sender.

Jake.

He'd been the best man at Lily's wedding, since Jake was great friends with Lily's husband and they ran a law practice together. Jake and I were friends, too, and had grown closer in the last few months. We'd worked on a few projects together recently when some of Trish's clients needed entertainment lawyers.

Jake: On my way to meet everyone now. Just need to take these gloves off first.

Kate: Are they your driving gloves, Jake? You're so fancy.

Jake: Yes. You found out my dirty little secret. I wear leather driving gloves while tooling around town in my Rolls.

Kate: How very dapper.

Jake: That's me. Dapper and dandy. Anyway, they're the boxing gloves because today has been a helluva day in the ring.

Kate: Ooh, tell me about all your fights. I presume you pulled no punches?

Jake: They don't call me the hard-ass for nothing.

Kate: They call you that because your ass is hard?

Jake: Oh, hey. You noticed my ass. Excellent.

Kate: I was simply speculating on the nickname.

Jake: Don't try to deny it now. You've been checking out the goods in the trunk. Understandable, since this ass is carved from stone.

Kate: Stone is cold and unpleasant.

Jake: Things no one says about my ass.

I inserted an eye-roll emoticon, then finished with . . .

Kate: Is there a list somewhere of things said about your ass? Admit it—you made that list yourself.

Jake: Don't need to. I believe you're that list's keeper.

Kate: Now you're the ass.

Jake: That may be true. In any case, I just finished birthday shopping with my sister for my mom, and I'm on my way over. I know you're counting down the minutes. I'd bet money on it.

Kate: You'd lose that bet.

Jake: Doubtful. Highly doubtful.

Laughing, I shoved the phone into the side pocket of my purse. I was *not* counting down the minutes until I saw him.

Or the seconds.

Please. I had other matters on my mind.

Even though the man did have a terrific rear end.

Not to mention a handsome face.

And a fast mouth.

Damn him. Damn all the what-ifs I entertained about him.

3

JAKE

My back was tight, my muscles taut. Hell, my mind had high-tension cables running through it.

That was par for the course for the last several weeks.

I left the office on a Thursday evening, the sun already set, the city lit with miles of neon, glitter, and glitz.

I drank in the New York skyline, the Eiffel Tower, the pyramid and its eye as the Lyft took me toward the Strip. A place I loved. Too bad it'd been a while since I'd enjoyed all this city had to offer. But this evening I was coming up for air.

It had been some time since I'd had a night out with my friends.

But first, shopping.

I tried to shed another long day as I headed to Caesars to meet my sister.

Christine had demanded my presence as a shopping companion, since our mom's birthday was next week.

After the driver dropped me at the massive hotel, I made my way through the casino, enjoying the sound of games and slots until I reached the stores, scanning for Christine. My sister leaned against the wall outside the perfume store, dressed in black, her brown hair piled high on her head, a pair of silver glasses on her face, looking every bit the badass businesswoman she was. She founded and ran Hamilton-Carey, a cruelty-free beauty products company that supplied several of the hotels on the Strip.

She narrowed her eyes above the frames, like she didn't recognize me. Staring down her straight nose, she acted as if she were seeing me for the first time. "Wait. Is that you? In the flesh? As I live and breathe?"

"No. It's my hologram twin."

"Ah, that makes more sense," she said. "I was thinking ghost, but hologram tracks."

"Fine. I'll play your game." I sighed like I was genuinely annoyed, but I wasn't. I was, however, curious what the smarty-pants meant. "What exactly are you saying?"

She studied my face, peering at my eyes, my nose, my ears too. She patted my cheek. "It *is* you. I just wasn't sure what you looked like. Now, I see you've aged ten years in these last few months."

I scoffed. "Thanks. Good to see you too."

She laughed, tossing her head back, having a blast at my expense. She slugged my arm. "Just giving you a hard time. It's been so long since I've seen you that I wasn't sure I'd recognize you," she said, gesturing toward the shop.

We entered the land of olfactory overload, a bright white store with too many bottles of eau du toilette. But Mom liked her perfume. And moms deserved whatever they wanted for their birthdays.

Mom had a collection of favorite scents, so here we were, looking to add to it.

"It's only been a few weeks since I've seen you, Christine." Defensive was my natural state of mind. "Don't you recall that I saw you when we were watching a Warriors game at your place with Carson?"

As we wandered past some celebrity scent created by a singer with only one name, Christine tossed me a skeptical look. "Hello? That Warriors game was three months ago. We watched it on Valentine's Day. And I live two miles away from you. You haven't seen your nephew recently either," she said, but there wasn't any accusation there. More like sadness, and that made me sad too.

Was she right?

My brow furrowed as I flipped back through the calendar in my head.

April, March, February.

Holy shit.

It had been a long time.

Too long.

Next to the Chanel, I bowed obsequiously. "Apologies, oh great sister of mine. I am a dick. Work has been insane. We had some new clients with all sorts of rights reversions, and it has been a hell of a crazy time." Business at the firm was good. Almost too good. In addition to the rights reversions, we'd inked new deals for TV shows and struck partnerships for on-air talent. Things were booming when it came to entertainment law.

And when I'd gotten into law school, I'd vowed to never complain about too much work.

Hell, I'd made that vow when I entered college too.

This was how I lived my life.

Christine and I knew all too well what the other side of the equation was like. We'd seen it happen to our dad growing up. Watched him struggle to make ends meet as an appliance salesman when we were kids. He'd weathered too many storms with zero business. Too many nights coming home without nabbing so much as a single dishwasher sale. I'd never bitch about having too much to handle, especially since all the extra work I'd taken on helped fund my parents' well-deserved retirement.

Dad's days with his new running club, training for a 5K.

Mom's time to garden, read, and relax.

And perfume. Lots of perfume.

Christine shot me a big-sister look as she squeezed my arm. "I know you have a ton going on, and it's awesome. No one works harder than you. But you need balance. You're working too much, Jake. I don't get to see you. Carson wants to see you. He loves his uncle. He asks about you, wants to know when you'll come by. He has a soccer game on Sunday."

That tugged at my heart.

I loved that rug rat. I wanted to see him, play pinball with him, shoot hoops with the kid. Christine's husband had died a few years ago, so I did my best to help out with her son, now eleven, when I could. "I'll pick him up after school tomorrow and play pinball with him."

Christine laughed. "I'm not angling for a school pickup."

"Too bad. You got one. And I will go to his soccer match this Sunday. I promise. Forgive me," I said, pressing my hands together in prayer as we wandered past an Obsession display.

She smiled, adjusted her bun, then shook her head. "No apologies necessary as long as you try to relax and take a weekend off. You need some downtime. Can you get away from the office? Relax? You seem tense."

"Should I book myself a spa getaway?" I asked, teasing.

But her gray eyes remained stern, knowing. "I mean it. Don't work yourself too hard. That's what Dad did."

"I'm not going to have a heart attack," I said softly. "Or nearly die of one either."

"Let's make sure of that. And that means doing something other than work. Can you just take a weekend off?"

I sighed, dragging a hand through my hair. "Maybe," I said, picturing the stack of contracts I needed to weed through tomorrow. But after that? "It's possible."

"Do it," she said, like a drill sergeant. "Have some fun. You're seeing your friends tonight, right?"

"Yep. We're hitting Edge in a little bit," I said.

"And that includes Kate?" Christine lifted a brow in question.

I stared at her inquisitively. Why did she single out

the gorgeous brunette? "She's usually part of the crew. Why do you bring her up?"

She smiled coyly. "No reason."

I crossed my arms. "Bull. You always have a reason. Are you running a secret underground perfume ring with her?"

Christine laughed. "No, but thanks for the new business idea. And, honestly, I've just noticed that you always seem to sparkle when you mention her."

I furrowed my brow. "I do not sparkle. I'm not a vampire."

Her eyes glinted. "But you know that vampires sparkle in *Twilight*. That's adorable."

"That's something everyone knows," I said, defending myself once again. "Also, I don't sparkle, period."

"Maybe a little sparkle?" She narrowed her eyes and held up two fingers, a sliver of space between them. "That's what I told my girlfriends. That you sparkle just the slightest bit. They all think it's endearing. A sparkly little brother."

I groaned. "Please tell me you aren't telling your friends about me and trying to set me up again."

She dropped her mouth wide open in a *who, me* gesture. "*Moi*? I'd never do that. I prefer to push you directly toward the women I think are best for you." She winked, then returned to her normal voice. "Anyway, I'm glad you'll see her. Like I said, you *light up* when you talk about her," she said, her word choice deliberate.

"It's not as if I'm a beacon of darkness when she's not around."

Christine peered at me again, then tapped my forehead with her index finger. "True, but if this work-too-hard routine keeps up, I'm going to order you some Botox, since it looks like you've aged ten years. And let's be honest, the ladies aren't going to be that into you as a forty-year-old."

I mimed stabbing my heart. "Dig the knife a little deeper, why don't you?"

She grabbed the imaginary blade and happily dug around in my chest with a wide smile that stretched to her eyes. "With pleasure."

"Has anyone ever told you you're sweet?"

She shook her head. "Nope. No one."

"That's what I thought," I teased as she grabbed a tiny bottle that looked Parisian. She held it up for my approval. The name said Come What May.

What the hell did I know about perfume?

Nothing.

But I knew sisters. And Christine wanted me to be involved in the gift-giving.

I took the bottle, studied it, sniffed it, and declared it fine.

"Great. Let's get it for her, and we'll give it to her next week." As we headed to the counter, Christine wagged her finger at me. "And when Sunday rolls around, I want to see that you've given yourself some *me time*, Kate or not."

I scoffed at the notion. Guys didn't need *me time*.

Yet, I definitely could use a break.

Maybe I was a little addicted to work these days.

And I knew the cost, had seen it in my dad. Only

recently had he started to prioritize health over work. While our situations were vastly different, I did need to be smart, to be cautious.

Trouble was, work was my natural state. The only way to not work was to fill the time with something else.

When I said goodbye to Christine, I made my way to The Luxe, thinking about how to keep busy.

My mind kept returning to Kate.

She's been on my mind more often than not lately. I wasn't sure when she'd commandeered her bit of real estate in my head, but there she was.

Might as well send her a text.

I took out my phone, tapping out a note as I walked.

We traded messages about bets and gloves and hard asses, and as I read them over, a smile tugged at my lips.

Maybe Christine was onto something.

Talking to Kate was always a good time.

And evidently, that was what I needed.

4

KATE

With a smile courtesy of Jake's texts, I popped open my lipstick tube in the ladies' room.

As I touched up the color, someone pushed hard on the door, and a gaggle of laughter followed as two women poured in. The bride and the maid of honor.

"You have to do this," the bride said, in that insistent tone women took with their besties.

"But this is *your* weekend," the maid of honor said, sounding apologetic.

"It's *our* weekend, Sidney. We're out of town. And you're single." The bride waved her phone around. "You need to have this hottie to get David the Douche out of your system."

Yup. Called it. The bride wants to sprinkle sex magic on the maid of honor.

I capped the tube and tucked it into my purse. In the mirror, the bride caught my gaze, asking me, "Doesn't Sidney need this absolutely divine man?"

Ah, the instant friendship afforded by the ladies'

room. "I'm going to need to see the goods before I answer that."

"Of course. Look. Just look." The bride shoved her phone at me, showcasing a picture of a man in a tailored suit. Chiseled jaw. Dark hair. Mesmerizing eyes.

"Why, yes," I said, "I'll take one of him too. Double serving. À la mode, please." The guy was a ringer for Henry Cavill.

"You *can* have him," the woman said excitedly, emphasis on *can*.

"Are you giving him away? Is he a party favor?" I asked with a laugh.

The bride laughed, too, and shook her head. "You can *order* Antony from Sin City Escorts."

Everything clicked.

This was indeed the *extra fun* kind of girls' weekend. The kind involving male escorts from the local firm that had made a name for itself in that department. "Good choice. Sin City has the hottest men in Vegas. And many are especially good at getting an ex out of your head."

"See!" The bride practically jumped up and down, then she turned to me and gripped my arm. "Her ex was a dick. He cheated on her with literally everyone in Phoenix. I want her to use this weekend here in Vegas to forget him. Doesn't she deserve this one?"

The bride thrust the phone at me again, showing off the hottie she wanted to order for Sidney.

Deserve.

That was a potent word.

Don't you deserve a girls' weekend?

Don't you deserve something special?

Don't you deserve this man?

That could work in some girls' night out marketing.

Sidney sighed longingly as she stared at the image, hunger in her eyes. Then she shrugged happily. "Why not? Throw caution to the wind."

That was one more thing you could lose in Vegas.

Worries.

"Toss that restraint out the door," I said in the spirit of things. "Use a condom, give consent, and then have the time of your life."

The bride grinned broadly. "See? She thinks you should do it."

"Do it," I said.

Once I left them to their adventures, my friends and I headed for Edge, our favorite club. A few minutes later, three men walked in, and my eyes arrowed right to one of them.

Tall, dark, and handsome Jake. Jake with the cocky grin and bedroom eyes, the hard body, and the just-right amount of confidence. Never too much. He was the Goldilocks of confidence.

My mind raced several steps ahead to a brand-new *what-if*.

What if he were an escort? What would it be like to order him up?

The man radiated not just sex appeal, but sexual intelligence.

Like he knew things. Deep, dark, dirty things.

Things I was damn curious about.

Like he knew the answers to all my what-ifs . . .

Except there were far too many complications to entertain those thoughts about Jake.

He was a friend, a business associate, and a white-hot distraction.

I hadn't the time or space for the latter.

Even though I couldn't shake the thoughts now that they'd begun.

5

JAKE

The second I walked into the club, I knew for certain what I wanted.

No. That was wrong.

It was greater than want.

It was what I *needed.*

The same thing I'd wanted for the last few months.

The same person.

Kate Williams.

In many ways, she'd been a mystery to me, and like in a good whodunit, I wanted to unravel her. Wanted to know what was going on in that gorgeous head of hers. She watched everyone, seemed to soak in details, to absorb everything she saw.

She seemed, too, like the kind of woman who knew everyone's secrets.

Did she know mine? That I fantasized about her relentlessly? About telling her what I wanted to do to her, whispering sweet, filthy words in her ear about taking her up against the wall, bent over the bed, right here, right now. Hard, deep, primal.

Anywhere, everywhere.

Lust was a gift, but it could be an out-and-out annoyance too.

Because the woman was, to put it mildly, hard as hell to read.

Despite the regular texting, she'd given no real indication she'd be game for more.

But sometimes I'd see Kate looking at me, checking me out, her eyes roaming up and down my frame. Fair play, I figured. I'd checked her out more than a few times.

More than a lot of times.

She was gorgeous, with lush chestnut hair, hazel eyes, and a face that could start wars—high cheekbones and full lips. Not to mention she had a stunning body.

But none of that would matter without her brains.

The woman was bright and clever. Unafraid to jump into any conversation, discuss any topic, toss out any question. That was the biggest turn-on of all—the boldness of her mouth and mind.

Yet, for the last few months, the time had never seemed right to make a move—for many reasons. We were friends, we had a burgeoning business relationship, I'd been as busy as ten thousand beavers, and, well, *the other one*.

Did she or didn't she? If she wasn't on the same page in the desire department, I didn't want her to feel uncomfortable or awkward. So, I kept my eyes open for cues.

Of the crystal clear variety.

I hadn't spotted any . . . yet.

Tonight, though, I had my Kate radar on high alert as I weaved through the crowds at Edge with my buddies.

Maybe they noticed I couldn't take my eyes off the brunette.

"Do you need some pointers on finally going for it with Ms. Williams?" The asshole remark came from my closest friend, Finn. He was also my business partner and, evidently, a mind reader.

"How did you know what I asked for from Santa for Christmas?" I went with sarcasm, the only defense when a friend could see right through you.

Adam clapped my back as we headed toward the women. "Bro, I don't even know if good old St. Nick has enough time on his hands to read that kind of sad letter."

Finn met Adam's eyes and nodded sympathetically. "It's clearly up to us to help our sorry-ass friend."

I rolled my eyes. "Gentlemen, has it ever occurred to you that the timing might simply not be right?"

Finn furrowed his brow and shot Adam another look. "Adam, has it ever occurred to you that Jake might be full of shit?"

Adam stroked his chin thoughtfully. "It has, in fact, occurred to me. Like, right now." He stared at me. "Just ask her out, man."

"You're missing the point," I said, because he was. There was no simple *ask her out* in this situation.

"No, *you're* missing the opportunity," he said, no sarcasm now.

His words gave me pause. Was I missing an opportunity?

But the conversation ended abruptly when we reached the women.

As we all caught up, I did my best to dismiss the peanut gallery's—both the guys' and my sister's—unsolicited romantic advice. But that proved damn near impossible because my mind was on Kate. And I was in the mood to spend some time with her.

Perhaps I needed to follow some of that unsolicited advice this weekend.

Soon Nina and Adam hit the dance floor, and so did Finn and Lily. That left me and Kate.

I flashed her a grin. "What's it going to be, Williams? In the mood for a spin on the dance floor or a drink? Or do you have a secret hankering to bet on the ponies?" She smiled as I made my opening offer to assess her interest. But before she could answer, I held up a hand. "Don't tell me. I bet it's the horses."

Laughing, she shook her head. "You'd be wrong." She glanced at the time on her phone. "I need to take off soon, since I have a meeting in the morning, but I can handle one round."

And that didn't bode well for my chances, but I wasn't going down without a fight.

"Door number two, then," I said. We headed to the bar and ordered gin and tonics, and as we waited, I asked what she was up to *after* her meeting tomorrow.

"Friday night, that is," I added, since that was the time on her schedule I wanted to occupy.

"Depends on how much work I have to do over the weekend."

I affected a shocked expression. "Work over the weekend? Say it isn't so."

"You're one to talk. Aren't you all work and no play lately?"

I lifted a finger. "*Was.* I'm taking the weekend off, per my sister's instructions. She made me promise I'd lay off the emails and contracts."

"And, being a good younger brother, you're listening to her words of wisdom?"

"But of course. And I think they should apply to you as well, Ms. Work All the Time. Make it a no-work weekend."

"Since you're doing it, I should do the same?"

"What a brilliant idea," I said playfully, then I snapped my fingers like I'd just thought of a grand idea. "How about you help me while away the next two days? Maybe some blackjack, or some glow-in-the-dark mini-golf. Hell, we could go to the movies." None of those options really felt like what Kate would want, but the suggestions might give my Kate radar a baseline reading. Besides, they were friendly options, and we were friends.

"Let me get this straight. You want *me* to go whack a ball, play some cards, or see a flick so *you* have something to do on your no-work weekend?"

I flashed her a huge grin. "Exactly."

"Dare I ask the next thing?"

"What's in it for you?" I supplied.

Laughing, she nodded. "Yes, since you seem to be lining me up to be your Sunday Funday plus-one."

"Why, I thought you'd never ask. One, it's on me. And two, I'm an excellent way to spend the weekend." If I kept the invitation light and easy, I'd be good. I wouldn't be pushing her in ways that might make her uncomfortable.

Laughing, she shook her head. "You're too much."

With an indignant huff, I answered, "Fine, we can do dinner too."

She knitted her brow, going serious in a second. "Like a date?"

I had no clue how to read her tone. None whatsoever. Was she asking about a date because she wanted the same? Or because she wanted to know enough to turn one down?

My radar was silent, so I stayed on the same path. "No. Like dinner. They serve food. You eat. It's good."

She stroked her chin. "Hmm. Food can, in fact, be good."

"See? Now you're getting the hang of hanging with me. I'll make sure you're well-fed."

"What more could a girl ask for?" Her expression shifted to focused, professional. "Seriously, though, it depends on how things go tomorrow. My schedule might be crazy busy, but if it's not, it would be fun to see you this weekend."

See you this weekend.

The radar beeped.

Faster. Louder.

Because those four words sounded like an opportunity of the golden variety.

We clinked glasses and toasted to friendship, as was our custom.

It fit. We were indeed friendly.

But tonight, I was feeling frisky, too, and with the *see you this weekend* in my crosshairs, I needed to take a shot. Maybe with a bet.

As I knocked back a swallow of my drink, I glanced at the dance floor. A woman in black leather sidled up against a man with sleeves of ink on both arms. They didn't touch, but they danced *at* each other. Yes, that was a perfect entrée, and I was going to use it.

"I bet they're grinding in thirty seconds," I said to Kate. She was a cat with catnip, unable to resist getting cozy with a wager.

She arched a playful brow. "You're only betting because you lost the last one."

"Please. *You* lost the checking-out-my-ass bet. Just admit it, Kate," I teased, shooting her a grin.

She shook her head exaggeratedly, like she was holding in a smile. "Nope. I was *not* thinking of your butt."

I scoffed, looking at my watch then at the couple. They were closer now, legs touching as they moved. They were easy to read. "Also, fifteen more seconds till the grind begins. That's my bet, and I'm sticking to it. You going in?"

She laughed, a happy, buoyant sound that I dug. "It'll take forty-five seconds."

"That's your prediction?"

She crossed her arms, like she was throwing down the gauntlet. "That's my guarantee."

I whistled my appreciation at her boldness. "You're confident. How can you tell?"

"From watching them," she said, a little coy, a little flirty.

She took a sip of her drink, then stared at the dance floor as the action unfolded. As if on cue, the woman in leather spun around, and the inked man yanked her to him, tugging her ass against his pelvis.

Forty-five seconds. On the dot.

"Impressive," I said, with a low whistle.

"It's my party trick," she said, like she was divulging a secret. And maybe she was.

I marinated on that bit of intel as I knocked back more of my drink. "Makes sense, since you're the Goddess of Observation."

Her gaze swung to me, her eyes blazing with curiosity. "Is that what they call me?"

She seemed intrigued, maybe pleased that someone was seeing her, reading her. "That's what you are," I said, sensing a chance. "You like to watch. To see what everyone is up to. In fact, maybe we should bet again."

She didn't answer right away. She lifted her drink, took a swallow, and set it down. "But you need to pay up first, mister, since I won the last one with my forty-five second prediction." A little sassy, she held out her hand like she was waiting for money.

I chided her, wagging a finger. "But we didn't bet for anything. We need stakes if you're trying to make me go broke, woman."

She tilted her head and surveyed the dance floor, her eyes stopping in the direction of a tiny blonde in a white dress making eyes at a hipster in skinny jeans a few feet from her. "Them," Kate said, with a subtle point of her finger. "I bet in one minute he'll have an arm around her waist, his hand on her ass. If it takes longer, I lose."

"And what are the stakes?"

"I have some ideas." She licked her lips, and as she did, a flash of heat crossed her hazel eyes.

That flash of heat sure as hell sent my radar pinging. That heat wasn't hard to read whatsoever. I moved closer. "Same here. And I know what we need to bet for."

"Tell me," she said, a little breathless.

I had an idea. A dirty, delicious idea. So much better than a spa weekend. "You want to know the stakes? You sure you're ready for them?"

"I'm sure." The two words were a challenge, and the way she returned my stare made it clear she wasn't backing down.

I sure as hell wasn't either.

Not tonight.

Not after my sister's advice. Not after the guys' comments. And definitely not after the earlier texts with Kate.

Flirty, innuendo-laced texts.

Texts that had made the radar listen in the first place.

Now it was shouting in my head.

And I knew what it was saying.

Opportunity.

I stared at Kate's lush, full lips. I took my time, lifted my glass, downed the rest of the drink, then set it on the counter. Stepping into her space, I swept a lock of her hair off her shoulder.

She trembled ever so briefly then tried to play off her reaction, to brush some unseen lint off her shirt.

Her shirt was pristine.

I went for it.

Because this was the opportunity.

And I wanted to let her know I took her to bed in my dirty dreams.

Did she do the same with me in hers? I'd been dying to know for months.

Only one way to find out.

Honesty.

"One kiss." It came out like a command.

Hell, maybe it was.

She stared at me, wide-eyed. She didn't look down, didn't back away. Simply held her chin high. "Are you truly betting a kiss?"

"Yes. I am." I clicked the stopwatch on my phone, counting the seconds. The room thrummed with music, bodies pulsing together, lips pressed, hips locked. The music seemed to vibrate in me too. My bones hummed as I pictured tasting her mouth for the first time. "Does that surprise you?"

"I suppose it doesn't," she said softly, but still loud enough for me to hear.

I inched closer, catching a faint hint of her scent, like

honey and almonds. "So, are you taking the bet, Williams?"

Her lips parted as she seemed to breathe in the night, the possibilities.

We had to be one of her possibilities.

Her tongue darted out briefly, a sign that maybe she was willing to take the bet.

But when she didn't say anything more, I gave her an out. "Or we can just pretend the bet never happened."

"Do you think I want to pretend it never happened?"

"You tell me," I said. This time I needed her to make the move. I had to know she wanted this—wanted me.

I held up my phone. The stopwatch on it ticked past one minute. The time she'd predicted it'd take for the couple to be tangled up together.

We both checked them out at the same time. The woman in white wasn't dancing with the guy.

Kate looked back at me and grinned.

Wickedly.

"Oops. It's been more than a minute," she said, lifting her chin. An offering. "Too bad I lost."

Her gaze darted around the club, and when she spotted a dark corner away from the dance floor, she led the way there.

I didn't need any more confirmation than that.

But I got it when she turned around, leaned against the wall, and locked her eyes with mine.

She was waiting for a kiss.

And she'd wanted to lose.

6

KATE

Just one kiss.

That was it.

That was all.

Didn't I deserve it?

Tonight might not be a girls' night out anymore, but if the maid of honor could have the Henry Cavill hottie, I could have one kiss as a bet.

I deserved just a little bit of dessert.

And Jake, holy hell, was he ever the definition of a decadent dessert.

Besides, maybe he'd stop being a white-hot distraction after one kiss.

It was possible.

As I gazed at his handsome face, his carved cheekbones, his square jaw, his eyes drew me in the most— dark brown and full of dirty intent. This man knew what he wanted. I saw it in those irises, so much desire, and it thrilled me to be the one he craved.

Thrilled me more than I was ready for.

Jake closed the remaining distance between us, clasped my cheeks, and dropped his mouth to mine.

The second we kissed, my skin sizzled.

My mouth tingled.

And my breath caught.

He swept his lips over mine, and in an instant, I *knew.*

His kisses were everything.

They were electric, hot, and heady.

Exactly as I'd imagined in all my what-ifs.

This wasn't the first time I'd thought about kissing Jake. And kisses were only the start. In my imaginings, they'd spiral into touching, shift into filthy words, and descend into games, make-believe, and scenarios.

I pictured it all with him ever since I'd started seeing him in a new light a few months ago.

He kissed me greedily, answering all my questions. For months I'd wondered how he would kiss. Would he be hard, tender, curious?

The answer was none of the above.

Jake Hamilton kissed possessively.

He kissed me with ownership.

With his lips crushed to mine, he *took* my kiss. He commanded my body. His long, tall frame pressed against mine and gave me nowhere to go. And I didn't want to leave. I wanted to feel everything in this moment. I wanted the sweet surrender to his lips. The scratch of his stubble. The taste of his breath.

This was a brief and wondrous escape from the troubles that had plagued me during the last year.

And what an escape it was.

Lips crushing, tongues skating, hands holding my face. As he consumed my kisses, my mind tripped back to how he'd read my wishes when he made his comments. *You're the Goddess of Observation. You like to watch. To see what everyone is up to.*

Did he sense the full extent of my secret desires?

That predicting when the couples on the dance floor would touch only skirted the surface of what turned me on most?

I loved imagining the sex lives of other people.

Imagining what others did behind closed doors. And, with the right man, I loved the idea of inventing scenarios for them. Talking about them. Getting off together to those scenes.

I was a voyeur of sorts. I'd learned this about myself from observing the people in this city, from my job, and from the books I read.

But I'd never practiced it. And now, with this sex-on-a-stick man devouring my lips in the dark corner of a club, I couldn't stop thinking about my particular brand of voyeurism. I trembled as I pictured taking this game to the next level with Jake.

To playing it.

We'd meet at a bar, find another couple to watch, and we'd tell the story of their kink—winding each other up, turning each other on, getting ready.

Would that couple over there like a sexy stewardess scenario? What about that one in the corner? Perhaps a handyman and hot housewife scene? Or those two over there? Maybe a boss-and-secretary game got them going?

Pleasure swept through me at the prospect of that kind of dirty storytelling with a lover.

As Jake kissed me hungrily, the reel in my mind flicked through images of all the games people played.

The game *we* might play.

Jake kissed like the kind of man who'd say yes if I asked him. He kissed like he'd be wildly aroused by taking me to a bar, only so we could turn each other on by watching others, by talking about their sex lives.

He was that kind of adventurous lover.

I could tell.

Because his kiss was so much more than a kiss. It was a prelude to dark and dirty nights. It was a kiss that spoke of one-night stands. Of hot sex with a stranger. Of sweaty bodies, passion, and the kind of wild trysts you could order in this city after dark.

I melted into his touch, giving in to the exquisite tension rising in my body, the lust radiating from where he pushed against me, making sure I felt the full length of his erection.

I did.

Dear God, I did. I felt every fantastic inch.

And even though I knew I shouldn't be doing this with him—a friend, a new business associate, a man I wasn't going to get involved with, because I *wasn't* going to get involved with anyone—I didn't want to stop.

Not at all.

I looped my arms around his neck, playing with the ends of his hair.

He liked that, judging from the rumble in his chest. The groan that fell against my lips.

He kissed me harder, rougher, and by the time he broke the connection between our lips, I was a hot, wet mess.

His eyes blazed with desire as he stared at me. The corner of his mouth curved up in a brash grin. Why did he wear such a cocky grin so well? I didn't know the answer, but I liked that he did.

He ran his fingers across my cheek. "As you can see, I always make good on my bets."

That was why he wore the grin well.

He knew himself, knew his mind, and that electrified me. I'd never acted on my deepest fantasies, because I'd never been with a man who had the confidence in his identity to go to that place, to play those games.

But Jake?

I'd bet he could. I'd bet it all on that spin of the roulette wheel.

And I wanted more of him. *All of him.*

My breath came quickly, my heart raced, and my cells cried out for his touch.

But I had a meeting to go to tomorrow.

I had business to tend to.

And stupid debts to pay off.

I brushed my hair off my shoulder, trying to act cool. I couldn't chance an entanglement. "I guess you did."

He pressed his hand against the wall behind me. "So, I believe you were about to say you don't have any plans this weekend and you want to spend it under me?"

Were we really going back to this? To the flirting?

I laughed hard. It felt good to laugh with him, even though the kiss had only been a bet, my willpower temporarily breaking down.

I straightened my spine. "I have to focus on the meeting tomorrow."

"Yes, I know. But the weekend comes *after* your meeting, Kate." He wasn't pushy. He was commanding and clear.

He made me want to ditch my plans for him.

But I needed my plans.

So I made a lateral move, going for a tease. "I thought we were going to the movies," I said ever so innocently.

"We can do the movies, or we can do plenty of other things." He toyed with the waistband of my jeans. Dear God, his fingers moving like that lit a new fire inside me. I was so damn hot and needy for this man.

"Such as?"

"For instance, we could deal with whatever *this* is." His eyes never strayed from mine.

"What is this?" I asked, nervous but wildly turned on too, as he seemed to see through me.

He moved closer again, ran a finger along my neck, down my throat, between my breasts, and into the V of my shirt.

"You know what this is. *This* is the last few months of tension between the two of us," he said, stopping to brush his fingers across the fabric covering my belly, making me shudder. "*This* is the way I want you. And the way you want me."

There was something so wildly alluring about a man

so straightforward about his wants and his needs. It was such a contrast to my ex, to the way he'd wanted to romance me, take me on dates, entice me with sweet seduction, and then used my good name to rack up all sorts of debt.

I didn't want to be fooled again.

But Jake? He didn't seem to be fooling me. He was simply being direct. Laying his cards on the table.

Sex and nothing more.

The trouble was, I had a mission, and that mission involved whatever Trish was going to throw at me tomorrow.

It didn't involve white-hot distractions.

With every ounce of willpower I could muster, I raised my chin and answered the sexiest man I'd ever known, the man I was sure would finally engage my fantasies. "As enticing as your offer might be, I really should see what my boss has in store first."

He brushed his thumb over my chin, his eyes darkening, his voice gravelly. "You know where to find me. And in the meantime, let me give you a little something in hopes that you'll reconsider my offer."

He leaned in, and then he pressed the softest, most tender kiss against my neck.

The bastard.

The fucking bastard. Because that kiss was like a taste of honey. A sweet little spoonful of ice cream. And as much as I loved the hard and heavy, a dangerous part of me wanted this sweetness too.

But I couldn't have it.

7

KATE

At ten the next morning, I perched in the black leather chair across from Trish Valentine. Her red hair was twisted high on her head in an elegant style, and her black glasses slid down the bridge of her nose. Over forty and stunning, the woman could command a room.

There were only two of us in here, but when she spoke, I listened intently.

She clasped her hands on her glass desk, flashed a smile, then began. "I can't wait to tell you about this project. It's a little bit daring. A little risqué. And you're perfect for it."

I sat up straighter, brushing my hand across my trim black slacks. "I'm ready."

"I hope you've been thinking about great girls' night out marketing strategies since last night. Because this one is going to challenge you in a whole new way."

"And why is that?" I asked, eager for my marching orders.

Trish took a deep breath. "Because we just landed a pitch with Sin City Escorts."

I blinked. That account had been with one of our competitors. The rumor was Sin City Escorts paid handsomely and offered lots of incentives. And people used the service extensively, as last night's ladies' room encounter had demonstrated.

I couldn't quite believe that we might net this golden goose and Trish wanted me to be the . . . goose handler.

Not that I was going to ask Trish if she was sure she wanted me to take it on if we won it. I wasn't some doe-eyed newbie or prone to polite modesty. Instead, I squared my shoulders and said, "I'd be happy to look after the account."

That pleased Trish, judging from her satisfied grin.

"Fantastic," she said. "Because they left their old marketing firm, wanting a fresh approach to the world's oldest profession. And I know you can provide a new take. You always think outside the box. You're a lifer here in Vegas, but you still look around like there are new things to see, new things to observe. I think you're going to surprise this potential client, and that's what I want—to surprise them. Because they're rolling out something new."

I edged forward in my seat. This kept getting more intriguing. "What are they adding to a stable that already includes the hottest men in the city?"

She smiled like she had an ace up her sleeve. "Indeed, their men are tops. But they want to expand their offerings."

Beyond the standard man-for-hire? "And what would that be?"

As if she was sharing details of a Christmas wish list, Trish said in a whisper, "They're testing out a new menu of role-playing."

Oh, my. That tickled my fancy. "They've never offered it before?"

Trish shook her head. "Not like this. Their female clients have generally ordered traditional escort services, which may or may not include sex—up to the clients." She waved her hand, airily listing them. "The boyfriend experience. A hot night out. Wedding dates, and so on. But that's starting to change. And now, Sin City Escorts wants something more . . . shall we say . . ." Trish spun in her chair and stared out the window as if hunting for just the right word.

But I had one ready, thanks to last night.

"Something more daring. Something a woman can give to her best friend. A present, almost like a secret," I said.

I'd had almost no details yesterday, but I'd been working on the concept, both while I was out with my girlfriends and later, on my own.

"Something daring," Trish echoed, trying it on for size. "Yes, I love that."

"I can see this as something women give each other." I dove into my concept headfirst, no timid wading in from the shallow end. "For girls' nights out. For bachelorette parties. For girls' weekends. Playfully naughty."

Her smile spread. "Exactly. Yes, that's exactly how Sin City will want to sell it."

"It's the ultimate gift to give your bestie." Thank heaven for the bride squad. I raised my hands as if showing off a marketing slogan in marquee lights. *"Don't you* deserve *the ultimate gift?"*

Excitement twinkled in Trish's green eyes. "I knew you'd nail this. Yes, the ultimate gift. The gift you deserve. That's a perfect starting point. Can you put together some more taglines, concepts, and strategies over the weekend?"

Could I?

Of course I could.

"Absolutely."

She leaned forward, shifting back to brass tacks. "I want you to think about role-play. Research it. Immerse yourself in the different styles. Figure out how exactly we can capture the essence of what a woman might want to order for a friend or herself. That's what we need to seal the deal."

"I'm on it."

She held up a wait-a-moment finger. "By research, I don't mean anything tawdry. You know that, right?"

Trish was always careful to respect boundaries. We might work for risqué clients, but she'd never ask an employee to do anything that would make them uncomfortable.

"I absolutely know that. I can research this online and in bookstores, no problem. And with my eyes."

She smiled, exhaling deeply. "Of course you can. You'll be fantastic. You're observant like a detective. Maybe circulate through the clubs and try to spot any other escort services engaged in role-playing. Bring a friend if you want."

"Not a bad idea." Be observant, like a detective.

Would Jake approve of Trish's assignment?

Jake and his hot kisses.

Jake and his confidence.

Jake and his offer.

But there was no room for Jake on the role-play marketing menu.

I didn't have the luxury of a no-work weekend. I had an all-work weekend.

Trish picked up a pen, tapping the edge of her desk. "Why don't you build off the ideas that you shared when we started—the notion of deserving a girls' night out. Spend the weekend researching it. We can meet for lunch on Sunday to review and see where we're at, ahead of the pitch on Monday, if that works for you."

"That sounds great."

"And before then, perhaps you could meet with one of the escorts."

My brow furrowed. Why would she suggest a road test when she just told me to stick to observation? "You think that's a good idea?"

"Yes. Try Antony. For research," she added with a smile, like she'd seen my confusion. "Just talk to him, I mean. Hear his perspective. It could be interesting, as well as helpful. He's studying for his master's degree in aerospace engineering, and he's interesting."

"Sure. Antony sounds great." I kept my voice even. Antony the escort-training-to-be-an-astronaut already fascinated me.

"I'll get you his info. You can hear from him about what Sin City's clients want, and we'll brainstorm how we can convey that. I want all the women who haven't tried it to say, 'That's what I want to get my best friend. This is the ultimate gift.'"

"It is," I said with a crisp nod. "Because it's a great gift."

"It's an all-I-want-for-Christmas kind of gift. A stocking stuffer and the ultimate naughty-list present rolled into one."

I laughed at how obviously she relished her part in providing these types of sensual experiences for women. She'd made me find the joy and humor in it too.

In a sweet, demure voice, I chimed in with "Dear Santa, I'd like a hot guy dressed as a police officer with a pair of handcuffs under the tree, please."

Trish's eyes sparkled with mischief. "Dear Santa, I've been so very wicked. I'm going to need a billionaire in a suit to put me on his lap and spank all the bad girl out of me."

"Dear Abby," I said, "is it wrong that when I go home to my family ranch for vacation, I'm hoping Mama has hired a hot new stable boy for me?"

"Dear Heading Home for Vacation, all I can say to that is giddyap, cowboy!" Trish dropped an imaginary Stetson to her head and pretended to ride off, snapping the reins.

We both laughed. Then she told me the bonus I would earn if we won the account, and I stopped laughing and nearly popped out of my chair.

It was enough to cover the rest of Damon's debt. It was a light at the end of the freaking tunnel, and I could hardly breathe through the excitement that threatened to bubble over.

"That sounds great," I squeaked.

She smiled kindly. "That should do it, right?"

I blinked. *Do it?* Did she know about my troubles with Damon? I kept those close to the vest, but she might have overheard a phone call. Or did she mean *do it*, like that would wrap up our meeting?

I wasn't sure at all, so I kept my answer ambiguous too. "Yes, of course."

It was a huge understatement. A bonus like that would put me free and clear of banks and headaches and hassles that I hadn't earned but had no choice but to shoulder. If I wanted good credit, I had to deal with the wreckage from my ex.

A few months into dating, Damon had moved in with me briefly, saying he was desperate for a place to live as he looked for a new job.

I'd wanted to help my sweet, romantic boyfriend, so I'd said yes, and for a few weeks, I'd shared my space with him.

Never had I intended to share my good name, but he'd helped himself to it, signed up for credit cards with it, and used those to buy watches, phones, and other goods he could quickly sell on the street.

He found a job all right.

As a crook.

Then he found a plane ticket out of the country and left me behind with all the charges.

Yes, it was fraud. Yes, he was responsible. Yes, I filed police reports.

But clearing that mess up with the bank takes forever.

His credit was ruining mine.

It was easier to pay it off now.

And with this bonus, I'd win the final battle.

I'd move on from him.

All I had to do was dedicate myself to this new project for Sin City Escorts.

I spent the rest of the day diving into a rabbit hole of fantasies.

When the clock sped into evening, I leaned back in my chair, turned to the window, and gazed out over the city, flashing back through the last twenty-four hours.

From Ava's new display that had beckoned me, to the bride giving the gift of an escort to her friend, to Jake's kiss and the wild thoughts that accompanied it, the last day had been . . . illuminating.

Then this morning had come Trish's news and her assignment, and hours of internet perusal. My head was brimming with thoughts, ideas, and concepts.

I had enough to go on to present a marketing plan in a few days for this new role-play service.

I understood the details, the ins and outs of how it would work.

But one missing piece nagged at me as I wrapped up for the day, shutting down my laptop.

How did it feel?

When you ordered up the role-play escort, how would it feel to play boss and secretary, to be the naughty criminal, to beg your teacher for a better grade?

When he left your hotel room that night, a trail of intense orgasms in his wake, how would you feel?

You'd feel . . .

I hunted for words but was unsure where to start.

If I was going to spark a potential customer's imagination, this was critical information.

I needed to know.

With that unsatisfying gap in my understanding, I said goodbye to Trish, left the office, walked past the Bellagio, and stood in front of the fountains.

I had always loved these spectacular cascades. Some of my most significant debates with myself had happened here—where to go to school, what to do about Damon, where to live in the city.

I'd talked here with my friends too, discussing life and love and the future with Lily and Nina.

The dancing water calmed my mind, the noise quieting my thoughts so I could listen for answers to questions that seemed unanswerable.

With the sun fading and night wrapping around me, I watched the water leap and fall in its beautiful choreography.

And this time, the path was clear.

How would a woman feel when playing a role in a sexy scenario she'd ordered up?

If I experienced just a taste of pretend myself, I would know.

Trish would never ask me to do that, but I could ask it of myself.

Because if I wanted to entice women to try this service, I ought to know what it was like.

I wouldn't need to order an escort. And I didn't need to go all in with acting out the boss and secretary or the naughty nurse and pervy patient. Direct experience wasn't necessary to deduce those feelings and generalize from one's related experiences—just empathy and imagination.

But I didn't think my plain vanilla lifestyle would pave my way to understanding.

Maybe something else, something closer to the target, would give me a bit of extra insight.

Call it a crash course in walking on the wild side, Kate Williams–style.

Alex, I'll take naughty fantasies for a thousand.

A mixture of some role-play and everything I've fantasized about for years.

What is *my dream dirty weekend?*

The water danced, and I grinned a private grin that sent a sizzle across my skin and a spark down my chest.

Yes, that was what I needed to nail this pitch—my version of role-play.

The music in the fountain swelled, the water rising higher, then higher still before it surged to its limit and finally splashed down.

It was hardly a subtle metaphor, but it was the perfect soundtrack to my thoughts.

Once I gave myself permission to indulge in this experiment, I immediately thought of someone to help me.

I gazed at the stars winking in the night sky as I considered the complications.

What about our tentative camaraderie? What about our group of friends, our business relationship?

But Jake didn't seem like a guy looking for something beyond the physical, like someone who wanted more.

I didn't either.

Sex would be enough for him. Sex would be enough for me.

I opened my phone and sent him a text.

8

JAKE

The silver ball slid down the board on a fast track toward oblivion.

That was no good. Carson was on track for a record score in the AC/DC game, but not if the ball went down the drain.

"C'mon," I urged. "Just slap that flipper."

Frowning in deep concentration, my nephew pulled on the flipper with everything he had.

The ball went screaming back up the board, smacking the lights, activating the jackpot round, and launching him into a new high score.

Adrenaline rushed through me, and I thrust up my arms in victory. "You're killing it, kid."

Carson didn't even blink. His concentration was epic as he plowed through the jackpot combinations. "Let's see how high I can go," he said, all intense and gamesman-like as he continued crushing it.

"Keep it up, buddy. Keep it up," I encouraged.

As the ball lolled, taking its time rolling back down,

he glanced at me, a grin on his freckled face. "You're like a cheerleader, Jake."

"You bet I am," I said, owning that title. "I'll bring pom-poms next time."

He laughed, then returned to the flippers, whacking the ball once again.

"Who's the man?" I shouted, pride gleaming in me.

"I'm not the man. I'm the master," he said, in a pitch-perfect imitation of me.

I froze, set my hand on my chest, and gazed heaven-ward. "Be still my beating heart. He's quoting me back to me."

Carson laughed and returned to the game, but soon lost.

He patted the machine, and I told him to pose for the camera. Grabbing my phone from my pocket, I snapped a pic and sent it to Christine.

She replied right away.

Christine: Corrupting the youth. I love it. Will he become a pinball master by age thirteen like you?

Jake: As long as he keeps learning from the great one. But truth be told, I think he's already there.

I showed the message to Carson, who smiled.

"I do think I'll be a pinball master soon. But what will you do when I become better than you?" His expression was dead serious. The stinker. I huffed like I was offended.

"This is the thanks I get for teaching you my finest skill? You're already planning to take me down?" I shook my head as I guided him with a hand on his back toward the snack bar of the pinball arcade. "I guess the apprentice is indeed becoming the master," I said with a dramatic sigh.

He patted my arm as we approached the counter. "It's okay, Jake. You can apprentice with me someday."

I pressed my palms together in an over-the-top thanks. "So generous of you. I am grateful you appreciate your elder."

He stared longingly at the cheese pie under the glass. "And I am grateful for the slice of pizza you're about to get me."

This kid. His sarcasm was top-notch. I loved it.

I ordered, and we sat down, chatting about pinball, basketball, teachers, and other topics essential to a fifth-grader.

As I spent the rest of the early evening with my nephew, I couldn't help but think that my sister had been right.

I'd needed time away from the office.

I felt lighter, freer. Physically less tense.

Time with this kiddo always set me at ease, reminding me of what was good in life.

Carson asked me to tell him again about my victory in the pinball championships when I was in middle school, and as he devoured one slice of pizza, then another, I regaled him with tales of my glory days.

He wiped the napkin across his mouth. "We should enter a competition. Together, as a team. I researched pinball. It turns out they have mixed-age competitions, so old guys like you and young guys like me can pair up."

I held up a hand. "Do you know I am thirty? *Thirty.* That's not old."

"That's old," he said matter-of-factly.

"It's not old."

"It's pretty old."

"You're just like your mother," I said.

"I'll take that as a compliment."

"Then take this as one too. I'd be honored to be your pinball partner," I said. "Also, I'm still the master."

He eyed me skeptically, then smiled. "If you say so."

As we left the arcade and got into my car, I was so damn glad that, for the first time in months, I wasn't mired in contracts.

Though a peek at my email told me there would be plenty waiting for me on Monday. The tension that had eased crept back into my shoulders as I pictured what I'd be facing when the next work week started.

But I remembered my business goals—help my parents with retirement and make sure I was all set too. As well as the personal one Christine had reminded me of—don't drive myself into the ground.

One glance at my pinball comrade told me the evening off had been worth it. Besides, I had no major plans for the weekend, so I could sneak in some of this work on Saturday morning, no problem. Maybe during the day too.

I dropped Carson off at his home and gave my sister a quick hug at the door.

"We had a blast."

"Thank you. He loves spending time with you," she said.

"Can't fault him for good taste." I winked.

"So cocky," she said, laughing.

"You say that like it's a bad thing." I ruffled her hair. "Love you, sis."

"Love you too."

I returned to my car, cycling through my Webflix options for the evening. Would I finish out that new heist series where the hero was racing against the clock to foil the world's greatest criminal masterminds? Or was I in the mood for something a little lighter? A new episode of *Spying on My Neighbor* had dropped, a quirky adult cartoon about a guy who was a naughty librarian and—wait for it—spied on the woman next door.

Or maybe I'd listen to a book.

When I turned on the engine, I toggled over to my audiobook, returning to *Educated*. I could get lost in a good story, and sometimes with this one, I wasn't sure I'd ever come up for air.

As I listened to the memoir on the drive home, I slid right back into the story, deciding that yes, *hell yes*, this would be my Friday night.

A book, some good food, maybe a workout, then an episode of a favorite show. Afterward, I'd crash and sleep hard.

I reached my condo on the Strip and headed inside,

pleased with my plan. But inside the lobby, my phone buzzed with a message.

The second I read the text, my mouth watered.

My skin sizzled.

My dick stood at attention.

And all my plans for beer, books, and sleep flew out the window. *Sorry,* Educated. *You're hard to beat, but this just did it.*

Maybe I was getting more than what I needed.

By the looks of it, I'd be having what I wanted too.

Kate: I'll take you up on your offer.

9

JAKE

Even though I was dying to know what had made her change her mind, the "why" could come later. As I stepped into the elevator, I asked the questions that couldn't wait.

Jake: Time and place.

By the time I reached my door, she'd given me the deets.

Kate: 8:30. The Rapture, that new club at The Extravagant. I hear the people-watching there is top-notch.

Jake: I'll be there. Will you have your field guide out, like a naughty research scientist?

Kate: As a matter of fact . . .

As my elevator shot up to the top floor, I stared at her last text, wondering what the rest of her sentence might be. She didn't continue, though, so I took the initiative and finished it. Because I had a hunch about what she wanted.

Jake: As a matter of fact, we'll be people-watching and more?

Kate: Yes. Does that work for you?

Jake: Anything works for me. Everything works for me. "More" works fantastically well for me. "More" is exactly what I want with you.

Kate: I had a feeling it might be.

Jake: And I have a feeling more works for you too.

Kate: Well, I AM asking you for it!

Jake: Yes, and I like your initiative. Let me tell you about mine. I plan on whispering filthy words in your ear as we watch others. I bet that works for you.

Kate: How did you know?

She wasn't coy or sassy. She didn't say, *However did you know?*

She seemed legitimately curious how I'd discovered the key to Kate.

And maybe the answer wasn't hard to find at all.

Perhaps I *was* good at reading her. Maybe this preference of hers was why she'd kept me at a distance for a while. Because she knew what she wanted from a man, but hadn't quite known how to ask for it.

Maybe she hadn't found the man who'd give it to her.

She'd found him now.

Jake: From knowing you. From how you are. From seeing those hungry, dirty eyes of yours and the way you watch people. From spending months trying to figure out what your particular kink is.

Kate: And you've found it.

Jake: Yes, and I've had my suspicions for a while. But it was clear last night when you threw down those bets. It was crystal clear when you watched those other couples dance. Your reaction gave it away.

Kate: What was my reaction?

Jake: Your eyes darkened, the skin above your cleavage

flushed, your breath came a little bit faster. You were tapping into your brand of voyeurism.

Kate: *whispers* I think I do have a voyeur in me.

Jake: You absolutely do, and it's hot as sin.

Kate: You like it?

Jake: Love it. And I loved figuring this out about you. Though I think you wanted me to figure it out. You might recall a certain day at the diner months ago when you said, "We all have different fantasies."

Kate: And you think that was an invitation for you to figure out mine?

Jake: I do.

Kate: Maybe it was. Maybe I secretly wanted you to discover it. Have you been thinking about this before?

Jake: In the shower. Late at night in bed. I think about what might get you off.

Kate: And what do you think it will be?

Jake: Tonight, it's going to be me. And it'll also be you finally getting to explore your filthiest fantasies.

She didn't reply right away, and as I unlocked the door and tossed my keys on the table, I imagined the look on her face as she read my text.

A touch of surprise maybe?

A widening of her eyes?

A knowing grin?

All of the above?

But her response surprised me.

Kate: Do you know what else happened that day at the diner? When I said we all have different fantasies, and then you said you wanted to find out mine . . . that's when I felt that first spark of attraction for you. That's when I started thinking about what you'd be like in bed.

Holy hell. I was an inferno already. This woman was bold, daring, and spoke her mind. *Finally.*

Forget being hard to read.

She was a book with the pages spread open now.

Jake: I cannot wait to show you what I want to do to your body. But I would love to know what made you change your mind.

Kate: That's easy enough. The meeting I had today. I have to market an escort service that's adding role-playing to its menu. I want to do an amazing job.

Jake: Ah, so you want to practice?

Kate: I do. But I also want to be up-front from the start. This thing we're doing? How about we agree to this: one weekend, no strings, no promises, nothing more?

This was better than a high score in pinball.

No strings sounded like my favorite kind of deal, especially since my last few attempts at relationships had gone up in smoke.

Two years ago, Cassidy had told me I was a shitty boyfriend because I was married to work. "You always put clients first," she'd said when we split.

Ouch.

That had stung because it was true.

But Debbie, my last girlfriend, was the reason I had no problem agreeing to zero attachments with Kate.

With my work schedule in the last year, I'd mostly just been interested in having fun with Debbie, and she'd said that sounded good to her too. Vibrant and carefree, Debbie loved to plan unusual dates—rock-climbing gyms, candy factory tours, laser-tag mini golf. We'd had a blast together, but after three short months of most excellent dates, Debbie changed her tune one afternoon at Red Rocks after we'd just hiked three miles.

"Let's get married," she'd said. "We can even do it this weekend."

Taken by surprise would be a massive understatement.

I had no empirical issues with commitment. I wasn't a devoted playboy, planning to swing his dick forever and ever. But neither did I want to sign up for a marriage license with someone I'd only just started dating.

Except that wasn't the only issue.

Her taste for fun stopped at the bedroom door. And I'd considered compatibility to be vital when it came to beliefs, passions, worldviews, and, yes, the bedroom.

When Debbie issued her ultimatum, I called it quits —with her and with dating for a while.

So, Kate's rules suited me fine.

Now I'd learn if we were as electric in the bedroom as I'd imagined we could be.

Tonight was no longer about *me time*.

It was about satisfying a woman who'd intrigued me for a while.

A woman I couldn't get out of my mind.

A woman I desperately wanted.

I glanced at the clock on the wall of my living room, the time a reminder that the games would be starting soon. I wrote back to Kate.

Jake: I'm about to get in the shower. While I'm naked, I'll be thinking of all the ways you want me to pleasure you. But I have one thing I need you to do.

Kate: What's that?

Jake: When I see you tonight, we're going to do more than watch and talk.

Kate: We are?

Jake: We're going to pretend too.

Kate: Ohh . . . tell me more.

Jake: We're going to role-play as we watch others. Think of it as a combo platter of your dirty dreams.

Kate: I like the sound of that. What's our situation?

Jake: We're potential business partners. We live on opposite coasts, and we're in town for a conference. We've been working on a deal for months and sending emails that border on flirty and dirty. We're meeting for a drink to seal the deal.

Kate: I bet the drink turns to something more.

Jake: Only one way to find out.

10

JAKE

She looked like a woman on the brink.

As I headed into the Rapture, wearing jeans and a sharp button-down, my jaw unshaven, her eyes were already on me from her perch on a metal barstool. She nibbled on the corner of her lips, appraising.

My gaze traveled up and down her body too. Up those long legs to the tight pencil skirt, down to those sinfully sexy heels, and up again to the tight short-sleeve top that clung to her curves.

All business. All sexy executive I wanted to put on her knees.

Dance music pulsed through the club, and her eyes stayed on me as I walked to her.

When I reached her, I offered a hand and said, like a professional, "Glad you could meet me tonight to finalize this deal, Ms. Williams."

"And you as well. Thank you for fitting me in, Mr. Hamilton." She sat up properly, a little demure.

I took the stool next to her, ordered a scotch, and

turned to look out at the lounge. It was teeming with groups of friends and couples, men and women already tangled together.

I returned my focus to her. "I'd been hoping we'd do this deal for some time now."

"I've been eager as well." She lifted her drink and took a sip, leaving an imprint of pink gloss on her glass. I grabbed her glass and knocked some back too, watching her eyes the whole time. The message was clear as I drank her vodka tonic—I wanted her taste on my lips.

"But this is an interesting choice for a venue to ink a deal," I said, glancing around, then picking a couple cuddled up on a chaise longue. The woman had long hair, and the man sported a beard. "It's not your typical business place."

She smiled like she had a secret. "I think the deals people are doing here are of a different variety." She nodded at the nearby couple. "Like them." Her breath came in a quick rush. "I bet they'll be going home tonight. Finishing the final terms in a hotel room."

Holy hell. She wasted no time. She went for it, and I loved how she jumped into the deep end. I took a swallow of my scotch, savoring the burn. "I bet she'll take his hand and lead him right over to the bureau."

I met Kate's eyes, and those hazel irises glittered with lust.

A new look for her. One I'd only seen last night. One I wanted to see all night long.

She let out a breath. "Do you think he likes to fuck her in front of the bureau? Standing up? Bent over?

Ready?" As the words came out of her mouth, her shoulders relaxed and she laughed.

But it wasn't as if the conversation amused her.

It was more like . . . relief.

Like she'd just said something she'd wanted to give voice to for a long, long time.

I inched closer, my shoulder against hers, our bodies aligned. I eyed the couple in question, the one we were using for foreplay. They had no idea I was using them to turn on this woman next to me. That was what made tonight so hot. "I bet she likes it when he fucks her against the table too. Bet she likes it when he bends her over the couch. Slides a hand up her back, grabs all that hair, and yanks hard."

She gasped. "She loves that. She might even go to the room first. Surprise him."

My skin heated up as she got into it. "Bet she wears nothing but a shirt. Takes off her panties. Bends over the couch, her ass in the air, waiting for her man." The image of *that*—not of the long-haired woman and the bearded man, but of Kate waiting just like that—sent lust barreling through my blood.

"She does that for him." Kate's lips parted, her eyes hooded as she gazed hungrily at the couple. "She waits for him like that. So he can feel how wet she is when he arrives. How much she wants him."

I slid a hand around her waist. I was dying to ask how wet she was. But I knew better. Games were games. Roles were roles. And in this game, we weren't talking about ourselves.

She trembled against my hand. "She wants him to

know," Kate whispered. Then she lifted her glass, taking a drink. "She wants him to know how turned on she is. She's squirming in her lace, and all she wants is to show him."

She turned her gaze toward me slowly, taking her time. Her cheeks were flushed.

Kate Williams had put all her cards on the table. Every last naughty one.

No bets, no bluffing—just desire.

I understood her wishes.

I understood how to fulfill them.

I tossed some bills on the bar. "I've got a room upstairs, Ms. Williams. Why don't we seal the deal in ten minutes?"

* * *

I booked a room so goddamn fast.

Handed her a key card. Kept one for myself.

Watched her go into the elevator.

Waited till she sent me a text.

She sent two images, and they made my pulse spike. This woman was masterful, and I strode down the hall, then waited for her signal.

It came in words and pictures.

A shot of her white panties on the floor, followed by her instructions.

Kate: Come find me.

A few minutes later, I used my key card to enter the room at The Extravagant, opening the door. The lights were low. One light flickered in the corner, and something that sounded like D'Angelo played from a speaker.

This woman had set the scene.

And she was one hell of a set designer.

The mood was sheer filthy perfection.

Then it was even better.

Because there she was.

Bent over the couch, blouse on top, nothing on the bottom.

And from head to toe, she looked so damn aroused.

11

KATE

The mind was a powerful organ.

Mine was overactive and had been all night. All month. All year.

I'd imagined *this*.

This was my go-to: the talking, the setup, the scenario. But I'd never set it in motion before. Given my choice to lay off men over the last several months, my body was primed.

My mind had provided the mental foreplay.

As I slid the key against the door, I already imagined the moment when he'd walk into the room.

How I wanted it to feel to him.

Peering around, I took in the space and decided to set the scene.

An ample living room was spread out before me, with a sunken area holding a large couch strewn with pillows. After putting my purse on the table by the bar, I headed into the living room, adjusting switches as I went.

Now the lights were low, seductive.

The plush carpet was inviting.

Not that a man would care one lick about the carpet. But I did. I was all about the mood.

I turned to a playlist on my phone—a low beat hummed from the device, a delicious soundtrack to seduction.

An image flickered in my mind as I pressed my hands on the back of the couch.

I pictured how *Ms. Williams* wanted her new business partner to find her.

Ready. Waiting. Aroused.

The latter was easy—I was more than aroused. My skin tingled with anticipation. My bones hummed. My God, I was doing this. Finally doing this.

I walked over to the bar, peered in the mirror, and pursed my lips. Grabbing my lipstick from the side of my purse, I slicked some on.

I turned around.

Unzipped my pencil skirt. Let it fall to the floor.

I shot a picture of it, sent it to Jake.

Feeling deliciously playful, like the type of woman who'd perhaps order a man to come to the room, I slid out of my panties with a sashay of my hips.

I took a snap of the lace on the floor and sent that to Jake too.

Or *Mr. Hamilton.*

My business associate.

Grinning, I returned to the couch and took my position.

I imagined Jake walking down the hall. That confident stride. The fire in his eyes. His tall, broad frame. I bet he was unknotting his tie as he went. My mouth watered at the thought of him tugging at his neckwear, undoing it.

"Jake," I said out loud, letting his name roll around on my tongue, letting it play on my lips. Ever since that first spark of attraction at the diner so many months ago, I'd wanted to know how it felt to say his name in the heat of the moment. To say it unbidden.

The attraction had only grown.

It expanded in my mind. It took over my dirty thoughts.

For the longest time, I hadn't known what to do with those feelings. Hadn't known how to fit them into my life, inside the walls that hemmed me in. So, I'd denied them. He'd flirted, and I'd darted and dodged.

But now I was giving in, fitting him into what I needed.

And as I gave in, I had my first answer to one of my questions—how would it be to say his name in a moment of longing?

Easy, that's how.

It was so damn easy to say his name with *want*.

As I waited for him, the full scope of my proposition shook me like the chorus of a rock song at a concert.

I craved this man.

I craved him from deep within my body and my mind.

For long, heavy seconds, the strength of those cravings scared me.

I had no room for longing, no space for anything more than knowledge.

Just stay in the moment.

Remember the mission.

Embrace it for what it is.

There. I was as ready as I'd ever be.

The moment began with a rustle of sound. Then, movement. The click of the lock. A rush of heat in my core.

The door opened. His breath hissed, then he groaned, low and deep. "Ms. Williams. I see you've prepared the final paperwork," he said. I thrilled at how he stayed in character.

"Yes, but I thought you might want to make sure everything is to your liking first." I turned my gaze to him.

Hell. This man was a sight.

He had indeed loosened his tie, and he tugged it off now, slow and measured, dropping it on top of my clothes. Raising one hand, he undid the top button of his shirt, and then the next.

"Actually . . ." He walked toward me, sounding as if he was appraising something, or like he was about to make a last, decisive chess move. "I have some terms and conditions."

"Oh?" My voice rose at this unexpected turn.

"Yes. Final points, if you will, that you'll need to meet."

"And if I don't agree?"

He bent closer, his lips near my face. "Then I walk away."

A shiver spread through me at his power play. "So, a loophole?"

"Yes, let's call it a loophole," he said, gently teasing.

"What's the loophole exactly?" I sounded breathless. I felt breathless.

He bent over me, his strong body pressed to my back, his stubble near my cheek, his scent—clean and masculine—drifting past my nose and intoxicating me. "With a bonus clause," he said, running his hands along my arms. His touch was exhilarating. It was tender and controlling at the same time. And his voice, so rough and husky, turned me on more with every word that fell from his lips. "If I make you come in the first five minutes, the bonus clause activates, and you get another one."

My entire body shuddered with anticipation. "That's bold of you. Are you sure you can deliver?"

He pulled back, staring at me with an arched brow. "You doubt me, Ms. Williams?"

I gave a coquettish shrug, which wasn't easy to do from that position, but it felt wholly necessary to the game we were playing. "Maybe I do, Mr. Hamilton," I said, a little tease. "After all, it's our first time doing business together. How do I know you'll deliver on all the terms of this deal?"

He stepped away, stood behind me, and lifted a hand.

I wasn't a submissive. I wasn't into being tied up. But a swat on the ass? Bring it on.

He brought his hand down hard on my flesh, and I cried out. *Loudly.* So damn loudly.

His expression was stony as he slid his fingers between my legs, testing me. I moaned as he stroked my wetness.

"Your body doesn't seem to doubt me," he murmured.

"True, but I still need more proof. Think of it as a show of good faith."

He gave another swat. Harder. Sharper.

"Ow," I called out as I grew wetter.

"There. Are you now convinced I'm serious?"

"Why don't you check?"

His fingers returned to my center, and I rocked against them until he pulled them away a few seconds later, bending close to my ear again. "Seems you're convinced."

"I think I might be," I said.

He took his time, drew a breath, and spoke in a filthy tone. "Then, can you agree to get on your knees and suck my cock once I've proven I can meet the terms on my end?"

"That sounds mutually beneficial," I said with a naughty grin. I ached to be touched again.

"Good." He stepped away from me, but never took his eyes off my body as he unbuttoned his shirt the rest of the way. I stared shamelessly, admiring the expanse of his chest, the cut of his abs, and the decadent dip of his V.

He smirked. "And are you enjoying the potential of our business deal?"

After months of dancing around my desire, I didn't want to pretend. I wanted to own this lust. "So much." I took a beat and licked my lips, our eyes locked on each other. "So damn much," I added, wanting him to know. "And you?"

His lips curved into a grin. "I find the possibilities of our partnership quite enticing." Returning to me, he brushed his fingers over the curve of my ass. I moaned as a wave of lust swept across my skin. "Absolutely, deliciously enticing." He spread his palm over my cheeks, squeezing.

"I was hoping you would."

He moved behind me, and I turned my face, following him, watching him as he stared between my legs. His eyes went darker, savage almost. "You see, Ms. Williams, I set those terms because I could tell how much you wanted this deal. But I'd also like to hear it from your pretty little mouth."

"I do want it," I said, breathless, desperate, and enthralled with our game.

"I want it too," he said huskily, as he put both hands on my ass, spreading my cheeks. "So goddamn much."

He kneaded my ass, squeezing, playing, groaning as he went, sounds of approval rumbling in his throat. With each touch, I grew hotter, the temperature in me shooting dangerously high.

I wriggled my rear, asking for more.

And he gave.

Oh God, did he ever.

His hand glided between my thighs, his fingers coasting across my wetness. My eyes fell closed. I dropped my face, and I groaned as he took his sweet time, indulging in touching me. "Oh, God."

He stroked my clit, his fingers expertly playing me. "Yeah, I think you'll meet the first term," he said, so damn casually, as he thrust one digit inside me. "I've got a feeling."

I had a feeling too.

Many feelings, and all of them were filthy and fantastic as Jake fucked me with his fingers. He crooked one inside me, hitting me in that spot that made my vision blur. That made the world around me narrow and spin.

My belly tightened, and pleasure crawled up my legs and pulled at my skin.

He followed my cues, thrusting harder, deeper with the quickening of my breath, the swaying of my hips.

Desire wound tight inside me, an exquisite ache that came before release.

I hadn't expected this so soon. So fast. But my legs shook, and I felt out of control. I was losing hold of my grip on this scene, on the game, on my goals.

I didn't think he'd take me so quickly, so commandingly.

As he fucked me with his fingers, his other hand banded around my waist, gripping me. He bent over my back, covering me, his stubbled jaw skating near my ear. "Yes, I bet we'll be doing this deal in many ways. *Multiple* ways," he rasped, and I shattered.

My hands curled around the couch, digging in, as the force of my orgasm tore through me.

I came like a wave hurtling toward the shore, faster than I expected, harder than I could ever have imagined, crashing more powerfully than I would have predicted.

My climax pulled me under as I moaned and groaned and shuddered.

I barely had time to surface for air when I felt something else.

Something I wanted desperately.

Jake's cock.

He rubbed the head against my wetness, stroking, teasing. Then checking his watch. "Looks like I met the under-five-minute clause. So it's time for the bonus," he said, then pulled back and grabbed a condom from his pocket.

"I do enjoy bonus clauses," I panted as my eyes locked on him, long, thick, and perfect as he sheathed himself.

He slid a hand up my back, pushing my blouse farther up, all the way to my neck. "Gorgeous," he murmured. "What a sexy back. I'd love to come all over your back."

I blinked. The image was so carnal, so arousing, that a fresh wave of heat surged in me. "You should sometime." My voice hardly sounded like my own. But it could only belong to me because I was saying things, doing things I'd only done in my dirty, very private dreams.

And I loved it.

I was awash in lust as his hand ran down my spine and between my legs again. He positioned himself, then in one swift move, he pushed into my wetness.

And I cried out.

I couldn't hold back my moans.

They were ridiculously loud as Jake filled me, and the delirious pressure made my skin sizzle.

He groaned, gripping me harder, thrusting deeper. His hands dug into my hips, and he held me so hard as he filled me. Then he pulled back, swiveled his hips, and stroked into me with a sexy grunt that sent heat across my body.

There was something so primal about the way Jake fucked me.

Something so alpha.

My blouse was bunched at my neck, and I wore only heels. He was still in unzipped slacks and his unbuttoned shirt, and he was fucking me like a powerful man fucked his woman at the end of the day.

With need.

With knowledge.

With control.

And with complete and utter desire.

He pumped into me, his hand traveling up to my hair, gripping my locks, wrapping a handful around his fist.

He seemed to sense that, for tonight at least, I didn't need flowers and candles. I didn't care for slow, sensual kisses all over. And I didn't need a ton of foreplay.

I needed good, hard fucking from a man who knew how to give a woman everything she wanted. Everything she needed.

Some days, a woman just needed to be bent over a couch and banged in a Las Vegas hotel room by a man who knew how.

As Jake rocked into me, his hands roaming around

my waist, palms reaching my breasts, a new under-standing hit me.

No wonder friends gave friends escorts for gifts.

Because this was a fantastic gift.

Hotel sex of the very best kind.

Hard, fast, powerful.

And out of my control.

This was what hotel rooms were for.

For being owned.

Being taken.

Being wanted.

I felt coveted as he stroked into me, his hands rough on my breasts, his cock deep in my pussy, his moans feral in my ears.

Moans of praise.

So fucking sexy.

Feels so good.

Yes, rock back on me, baby. Take me deeper.

All those words turned me on higher, made me lose myself in this world of night, of fantasies, of games made real. Jake fucked me like my business partner who wanted to have hot, dirty hotel sex with me.

Soon, I felt that pulsing again—another climax tugging me under.

"Mr. Hamilton," I cried out, grasping at our game, trying to hold on to it, but losing myself in sheer bliss.

"Yes, give it to me."

I was already there, soaring, flying. Feeling so much. He fucked me to the limits of my pleasure and his too, as he grunted and groaned through his own release.

Sounding exactly like a man in a fantasy would.

A man who was exploring my fantasy.

And I realized something terrifying—this was everything I'd hoped it would be and more.

That was what scared me.

The *more*.

12

JAKE

A man should never ask *How was it?* after sex if he doesn't know the answer. If you can't tell whether your partner liked it, then you're not going to get the answer you want.

You'll get a hem and a haw.

A lie.

A smile that covers up her lack of orgasm.

The only reason a man might ask a woman *How was it?* would be to give her a chance to purr in the afterglow.

After we cleaned up and disposed of the condom, I scooped Kate into my arms.

"Why are you carrying me?" Her question was genuine, but she laughed as I crossed to the bed.

"Because it's fun." I dropped her on the mattress, eliciting a sarcastic *"Thanks."* But her expression said she was in a playful mood.

Like me.

Good sex always puts me in a better mood.

Great sex, and that was what we'd just had, was a happiness elixir. I was a king right now, riding the best kind of high.

I flopped down next to her, my body still craving nearness to the woman I wanted. Shifting to my side, I ran my fingers along her cheek and asked the question, because I couldn't wait to hear how she answered. "So, how was it?"

When she met my gaze, her eyes were soft and pretty, a hint of vulnerability in them. Or perhaps it was openness. Whatever it was, I liked it, especially as she asked gently, "You don't know?"

I stroked her arm, savoring the feel of her warm skin. "I want to hear it from you."

Her eyebrows climbed. "You do?"

"Why so doubtful?"

"It doesn't seem like you to conduct a postmortem on what was obviously great sex."

Ah, that description warmed the cockles of my heart. And other cockles. "But it's exactly like me, and here's why—I like fucking you. I intend to fuck you again, and I want to make you scream in pleasure every single time. So the more you tell me, the better it gets. Is that good enough for you?"

She smiled like the Mona Lisa. "All you had to do was say that."

"Does that surprise you? That I want to know what feels good to you?"

She shrugged. "A little, to tell the truth."

"Why is that surprising?" Then it hit me—the same reason most women weren't used to this conversation.

My jaw clenched. "Let me guess. Guys you've dated didn't ask or care how to make sex better for you? Or if there was anything else you wanted to try?"

She tapped her nose. "Bingo." She ran a hand through her hair. "Sure, some asked how I liked the steak. Was it cooked the way I wanted? But no one asked if I wanted chicken. Or pork. Or the vegan patty, perhaps, with sriracha sauce."

I laughed at her outrageous metaphors. "Or sautéed tofu?"

"Exactly. Didn't they know I wanted bacon-wrapped gizzards one night and garden burgers the next?" She laughed, then her humor tapered off. "But seriously, that was exactly how it went. No one asked. No one wanted to know, I suppose."

Shoving a hand through my hair, I huffed, then tried to let go of my frustration. I would never understand why jerks appealed to women. "Enlighten me. Tell me what draws you to the breed of man known as 'jackass.'"

She pushed my bare chest. "I didn't say I liked that breed. That's not my thing. I don't go for cocky assholes. But news flash—most men don't know how to make sex better for a woman. Because most guys don't actually want to try new things."

I propped my head up higher, liking this direction and curious about what she might share. "So, this was new to you?" I waved toward the living room. "What we did?"

She inhaled like she was drawing strength, then nodded. "Yes, role-playing like this is new to me."

The warmth that spread through me was different

than lust, stronger. Kate had let me in on something private and personal, and my heart sat up and took notice. "But you've wanted to? And were never with someone who did too?"

"Exactly. I've never met someone I wanted to explore those aspects of my sexuality with. I think I always knew I wanted more than vanilla sex, more than reverse cowgirl on anniversaries, but I didn't know exactly what I did want either. I didn't know if my interests were in role-playing or voyeurism or just trying some new positions and having sex on the table or something."

"How did you figure it out? What you craved after dark?"

She took a beat, glancing around the suite, which felt like a private cocoon now. "It took a while. In college, sex was usually just about the freedom and novelty of being able to have it in your dorm room instead of sneaking around. Then after college, I was so focused on business that all that took a back seat. Once I started dating more seriously, I didn't quite realize what I was missing, either, because I was always drawn to the really romantic guys."

I cocked my head. "That's surprising. You don't seem like the type who likes to be wined and dined."

"I like those things," she said softly, like she was letting me in on another secret.

I held up my hand to halt her right there. "Whoa. Stop the presses. Kate Williams likes to be romanced?"

She rolled her eyes. "And you wondered why I didn't want to say anything."

I ceased the teasing, tucking a strand of her hair behind her ear. "It just doesn't seem like you, that's all. You come across as so tough. Take no prisoners. Like you don't need flowers or dinners at Michelin two-star restaurants."

Her eyes lit up. "I love Momofuku."

"So that *does* get you excited," I said, teasing her more gently. Also, I could relate—that was a damn fine eatery, the best in this city, and a classic date place. "So, secret romance-lover, why do you pretend you're not into romance?"

She sighed heavily. "Because of my ex. He was a full-on romantic, and I was kind of swept up in that. A lot swept up in that, actually. But then he opened credit cards in my name, took off, and dumped all his debt on me. Fabulous, isn't it?"

I sat up straight, spurred on by surprise and outrage. "Are you kidding me?"

She shook her head, her expression strong but resigned. "I wish."

I snarled. "That's terrible."

"I agree, but it is what it is. I've been working my butt off to repair my credit, and I'm almost there. But the whole thing made me wary of relationships and romance."

"I can't imagine how hard that would have been," I said sympathetically, lying down again and running my fingers along her arm. Like a book I'd opened, the pages of Kate were coming into focus, and I understood the root of her reluctance. "You said you had a vague idea that you might want to spice things up—when did you realize it for certain? With your douchey ex?" I braced myself, clasped my hands, and muttered a prayer. "Please say no, please say no, please say no."

I was joshing with her, but spoke the truth. I hoped to hell that jackass didn't get to see this side of her.

"No. Not with him."

I exhaled, relieved. "Good."

"It is good. And honestly, that wasn't our vibe. It wasn't like him to ask what turned me on, what I wanted from him. He assumed it was flowers and candles, and while I do appreciate those, don't get me wrong, I began to realize from the books I was reading, from the fantasies I was having, that I wanted something else." She ran her fingers down my chest, and for a second, maybe more, it felt like she was subtly saying I was that something else she wanted. And I liked being that something else.

"Did you ever tell him?" I asked, tensing, hoping again she'd say no.

She shook her head, then pursed her lips. "No. But I'd intended to. I trusted him, so I'd been planning to let him in and share some of my fantasies with him." She took a breath, playing with the hair on my chest. Once she steadied herself, she met my gaze. "But I'm glad I kept those to myself. I'm glad I never shared my fantasies with him. I feel like I kept a more important piece of myself than the money I've had to pay. Money can be replaced. Fantasies—you don't want those corrupted."

I lay back down next to her, absorbing what she'd just said. "Fantasies are a gift. Letting someone in, sharing with them—that takes an enormous amount of trust. I can understand why you're glad you didn't give those up to someone who would never understand how precious they are."

A smile tugged at her lips. It was so damn endearing, the way the smile seemed to own her. "They are precious. They're part of what makes you tick," she said.

Stroking her hip, I pressed on. "Why did you tell me?"

Her grin widened. "You sort of guessed them, Jake."

My brow furrowed. "Is that the only reason you told me? Because I took a good guess?"

She swallowed, her expression shifting to a serious one. "No, that's not the only reason why I told you." The way she said it, quiet and from her heart, seemed like a prelude to a confession.

"Then why?"

Her gaze drifted away, and she stared at the ceiling, like she was lost in thought. Finally, her focus returned to me. "Because I could tell you didn't want to trick me. Because you've been up-front about your interest."

I arched a skeptical brow. "I didn't make a move on you until you gave me the green light."

She chuckled like I'd made a ridiculous claim.

"Hey," I protested. "C'mon. I was a gentleman."

Another laugh from her, then she collected herself. "That's true, but you've been pretty flirty in our texts— like, for the last few months. And not just in texts. In person too."

"Damn. I thought I'd been a good boy, waiting for clues."

She tap-danced her fingers up my chest. "Maybe you were, but I had a hunch which way your detective work was headed."

I scoffed at myself. "Guess I wasn't as subtle as I thought." Then I shrugged because it had all worked out in the end. She was here, nearly naked, and just a few minutes ago, she'd been screaming my name. "But since the cat's out of the bag, let me just say—I've wanted to get you naked for a while now."

"And maybe that's part of why I told you my fantasies and why I haven't done this with anyone else. But most of all, I told you because I knew I could trust you."

That got my attention and then some. "How?"

"Because Lily trusted you," she said, her tone intensely serious.

I ran my hand along her hipbone. "She did. And with good reason." I took a beat, wanting to ask something important. "Does it bother you knowing what went down?"

She shot me a grin. "You mean the fact that you've been with my best friend? Well, you were the back half of a manwich."

I cracked up at the blunt way she put it. That was precisely what I'd done for Lily. The laugh spread through me, settling into my gut, my bones. Kate chuckled deeply too, her shoulders shaking.

But when we both settled down, I returned to the topic. "Does it bother you?" There was no reason to skirt around the truth. Kate had played a critical role in engineering Lily's ultimate bedroom fantasy—Lily wanted two men to take her at the same time, both men pleasuring her and only her.

She and Finn, now her husband, had asked me to do the honors.

It had indeed been an honor.

And a hot-as-sin night, taking care of Lily and satisfying her dirty dreams at the same time.

"No," Kate answered. Far from awkward, she seemed relieved I'd asked the question. "I like it, actually. It says something about you. It says you're trustworthy. It says you value the kind of love Lily and Finn have. It says you understand fantasies and desires, and you respect them. It's far too easy to assume fantasies are just about sex."

I scoffed. "Fantasies are about much more. It's about this." I tapped her forehead. "It's about who you are."

"Exactly," she said, alight with energy and animated. "And that's why I told you what I wanted tonight. That's why I wanted to try this out with you. Only you."

Only you.

Were there any better words than those?

Not at this moment.

Not between a man and a woman in the bedroom.

Between lovers.

And for now, Kate was my lover, a role that suited her. That suited me.

I growled my appreciation for her answer, and the sound radiated deep inside me. "Good. Because I'm going to be totally honest here—ever since what happened with Lily and Finn, I've wanted to know what made *you* tick."

Her gaze never left mine. "Why is that?"

"Because of the way you got involved. How you suggested me and played a part in making that happen for your friend. It made me curious about you."

She gave a sweet smile. "Because I'd seemed vanilla to you then?"

"A little, yeah," I admitted.

"And then I suddenly seemed kinky?"

My fingers found their way to her hair, and I ran them through it, savoring the silky feel of the strands almost as much as I savored this chance to get to know her more. "Yes. And I liked your kink. I liked that you wanted to give her a fantasy. It said you were open to trying new things."

She scooted closer, leaning into my hand, my touch, almost as if giving in—to me, to this fantasy, to this aspect of her sexuality—in a whole new way. "And that's *your* kink? Trying new things?"

I shook my head, still playing with her hair. "Not at all. But you're close."

"What is it, then?"

"Guess," I said with a grin.

She surveyed me up and down. "Hmm . . . what is Jake's kink?" She tapped her chin, her brow still furrowed. Then her eyes twinkled, and she dropped an imaginary mic. "Making a woman scream in pleasure."

"Boom." I moved down her body, pushed up her shirt, and buried my face in the valley of her breasts, sucking on a nipple till she cried out in a long, sexy moan. "*Jake.*"

I let go and grinned wickedly up at her. "Making you

moan like that is my thing. It's my kink. It's what gets me going. It's what makes my dick hard, and what makes my mind sharp. I find nothing hotter than turning on the woman I find attractive. And you, Ms. Williams, are the woman I'm wildly attracted to."

A tremble moved down her body. "You're the man I'm attracted to," she whispered.

"About time you admitted it," I said.

She swatted my chest. "Well, since you're being blunt, I will be too. I wasn't even attracted to you before your manwich."

I groaned, pulling a pillow over my head. "You're killing me."

She tugged the pillow away, propping herself on an elbow and staring hard at me. "You say that like it's a bad thing."

"You're sitting here half-naked, telling me about the time you didn't find me attractive."

Rolling her eyes, she straddled me and pinned my wrists. "I'm saying I saw you in a different light after you did that for Lily and Finn."

My dick twitched at her words. "You did? Like you figured I was a sexual giver?"

She nodded, mischief in her eyes, her lips curving up as she subtly rocked her hips against me. "I didn't expect that to happen. I didn't see you that way at first. Empirically, I knew you were handsome, but I didn't *feel* it in my body until then. Because what you did took a lot of guts and a lot of confidence."

I rolled my hips up against her, letting her know what she was doing to me. "And that aroused you?"

Her voice went husky. "Confidence is such a turn-on. And you had so much of it. And then the morning after, at the diner, I saw you in a new light. As this wildly sexual creature."

Best. Compliment. Ever. "Please make me a plaque saying that. Jake Hamilton, Wildly Sexual Creature."

She seemed emboldened, sounded awestruck. But it was also as if talking had unlocked something inside her. Like she was free to share these thoughts for the first time. "I started to wonder what you'd be like in bed. What you'd say. How you'd handle my fantasies."

I liked where this was going. "Do you ever fantasize about me?"

She nodded. "I do. I have. So many times."

A groan worked its way up my chest. My dick was ready to go again and again and again. "That's so fucking sexy. Tell me more, baby. What did you think about us? What did you picture us doing?"

She seemed lost in her world, enrapt in sharing as she moved her body back and forth. "I imagined the things we might do. The roles we might play. I wondered if you'd like them. Get into them."

Gripping her hips harder, I rocked with her. "And your answer was yes?"

"The more I thought about you, the more it seemed like a yes."

No wonder I'd been fascinated with Kate for the last several months. We'd seen the same thing in each other. "Kate," I said, gravel in my voice.

"Yes?"

"The reason we've been flirting? The reason we've been trying to figure each other out?"

"Yes?"

"It's because we were reading lust and attraction in each other. We were seeing desire and need."

She let out a sensual moan. "I think we were. I think we were dancing around it for months until last night."

"And now we're having it."

Her gaze locked with mine. "I want to have it again. I do. I really do."

"Ask, and you shall receive," I said, stripping off her blouse, getting her fully naked at last.

She pushed my shirt off the rest of the way, and it felt like a new level of intimacy.

I moved from under her to shed my pants and boxers so we were both down to nothing.

That felt fitting.

Here I was with this woman who already intrigued me, and she had given me all the more reason to find her compelling. Because she wanted to experiment. Because she wanted a man to trust. A man to give her pleasure.

And there was nothing—nothing on heaven or earth —I wanted more than to give her that.

I brought her back on top of me. "You deserve to feel good. You deserve all the pleasure in the world," I told her.

"I want it. I want it from you," she whispered.

Grazing a hand down her body, I played with the hair on her pubic bone, then spoke low and dirty. "Mr. Hamilton would like to see you on his face right now.

Fuck my face till you see stars, and that'll activate the bonus clause one more time."

Her eyes seemed to roll back in her head, then she licked her lips, glided up me, and in seconds, I'd pulled her sweet, hot center to my mouth, groaning the moment I made contact.

Once she started moving, her mouth did too.

The words that fell from her lips told me that this was one of her fantasies.

She fell right back into her role, rattling off Ms. Williams's thoughts.

I thought about this while we were signing the deal.

In the conference room, I was squirming.

Picturing this as we reviewed the paperwork. Right then and there. Climbing you. Riding you. Oh God, riding you just like this.

As I licked and sucked her sweetness, her sentences grew choppy, short, and her words became incoherent sounds.

I was in dirty heaven too, doing my favorite thing in the world—making a woman feel spectacular.

But not just any woman.

This woman.

The one I'd pictured. The one I wanted to know. The one I was getting to know tonight.

I was learning her secret wishes.

Learning I was part of them.

And hell, that made electricity crackle in my veins.

It made my whole body sizzle with lust as I devoured her pussy, taking her to the edge.

She detonated, coming hard on my face, tasting like sin and desire.

She was the woman who knew my mind too, because when she slid down my body, she took me in her mouth and sucked me off till I was nothing but lust and filthy bliss as I came hard, my world spiraling away into a blur of pleasure and release.

After, I murmured something like "We should go. I should go."

She voiced the same thing. "I should go too." But she curled around me as she said it, and actions spoke louder than words.

Ours said we were staying.

That didn't fly with my plans for this weekend, or hers.

But we did it anyway.

13

KATE

I woke with a jolt as the sun streamed in.

"I have to go," I said, scrambling out of bed to make my meeting.

"See you tonight, Ms. Williams. I'll send your assignment later," Jake said, all raspy and sleepy-sexy.

I brushed my teeth, and he fell back to sleep quickly. On my way out of the bathroom, I sneaked one last look at him in bed, the sheets sliding low on his hips. When I'd left the bedroom, he must have shifted because they'd slunk down farther, showing off the curve of his ass.

"More," I murmured, as if I were devouring a piece of delicious cake.

Because that was quite possibly the sexiest sight ever —Jake sleeping soundly with his gorgeous carved back and ass on display.

As I left, I sent him a text.

Kate: Fine. I'll admit it. Your ass is spectacular. I snagged a lovely view of it on my way out. It's hard and firm, and I just wanted to bite it.

Then I pushed thoughts of him away as I headed home, showered, and made it to my meeting in the nick of time.

* * *

I'd done plenty of background interviews as part of my job. But none had ever been with someone this good-looking.

Or this interesting.

I found Antony fascinating as I questioned him over coffee about his decision to enter this business.

His brow pulled, and he hummed thoughtfully. "Was it a hard decision to become an escort?" he asked, repeating my question, then he shook his head. "Not at all. I've always enjoyed the company of women. Women are fascinating, sensitive, easy to talk to. Sure, at first I was drawn to it with the endgame in mind."

"Your master's degree?" I confirmed as I took a sip of my English breakfast tea.

"Yes, and graduate school is not cheap. So I had to make a choice—take out loans or earn enough on my own. But it wasn't a difficult choice. I meet women from all walks of life, with all sorts of personalities, wishes, aspirations. Every woman I meet, I learn something from—humor, kindness, a new word or phrase, a type of cuisine, an approach to the world. I'm lucky to be able to do this for a living."

"You're like a therapist, lover, friend, and companion," I said.

"Indeed. In many ways, I am. I get to wear many hats. And take off many hats," he said with a wink.

"You enjoy it."

"I do."

"It almost sounds like you might want to keep this job after you finish your engineering degree," I said with a curious smile. "Do you?"

He shrugged happily. "I might, but that could be challenging. We'll see."

"With an aerospace degree, are you hoping to be an astronaut?"

He laughed lightly, like that was an impossible dream. "No. But I would like to build rockets. And this helps make it happen." He flashed a winning smile, the kind of grin that melted panties and made women drop a cool grand for a night with him.

And that was what the bride had paid for her maid of honor, Sidney, to get lucky. It was an odd realization, sitting across from this *GQ*-esque man, knowing who he'd slept with the other night.

I briefly wondered if Sidney got everything she needed from him. I hoped so. *You go, girl—more power to you.*

I cleared my throat, preparing to segue into the main reason for this get-together. He'd talked about being an escort, but I needed to understand more of his mindset while on the job.

"This may be personal," I said, running my finger along the rim of my mug, "but Trish said you'd be willing to talk about it, and I'd like some insight to plan how to best market the service. Does it feel like work? And how do you make a woman feel special? Or whatever it is she wants you to do?"

He hummed, like he was considering the question, then leaned forward. "Forgive me if I am too forward. But have you ever been with someone who made you feel spectacular?"

A blush crept across my cheeks in seconds. I heated up thinking of last night, of the things Jake and I had shared. Not only the otherworldly sex, but the conversation and then the cuddling. Who knew Jake was a cuddler? But he was—the best kind. All warm and snuggly, spooning me perfectly, brushing gentle kisses against my neck.

But I couldn't entertain those notions. I had to focus on work, since that was what this weekend was about.

Everything I was doing was for work.

Only for work.

And work included Antony's piercing question. Had I ever been with someone who made me feel spectacular?

"Yes, I have," I answered.

He smiled. "Good. Everyone should know what it's like to feel amazing. And that's what I want to do for the women who are kind enough to hire me."

Kind.

Such an unusual word to use in this field.

"Why do you want them to feel that way?" I asked.

His dark eyes were intense, passionate as he answered. "Because when they book me, they believe I can bring them what they want for a night. That I can deliver companionship, pleasure, friendship, a shoulder to lean on."

"Admirable goals." For a brief moment, I let myself linger on how that might feel. The past few months, I'd been so nose to the grindstone, so focused on *my* endgame, that I'd deliberately avoided intimate companionship and the friendship that could come with it. But hearing those words from this man, whose job was to deliver them, made me crave those things just a bit.

Companionship, pleasure, friendship.

That didn't sound so bad at all.

Maybe someday.

"You might call them admirable, but those are basic human needs, as I see it. And when a woman requests me, I have the chance to give that to her. That's an honor, and I don't take it lightly. I want every woman to feel spectacular."

I let that marinate for a moment as the espresso machines whirred behind us. "Every woman should feel spectacular," I said, trying that on for size. It might work as a slogan.

His eyes twinkled. "Yes. Exactly. That's my mantra. I want the women I'm with to feel like sexy angels."

"Do you make them feel that way?"

He nodded. "I believe so."

"Do they all want sex?"

He shook his head. "Less than half, actually. There was a client this week who simply wanted someone to talk to. That's what I gave her. I listened, and she was worth it. She had a lot on her mind and heart."

I wondered if that was Sidney, but it wasn't my business to ask.

Antony and I spoke for a bit longer, and I thanked him when we finished and then watched as he left, admiring his frame, his physique, and his kindness.

Funny, how you didn't think of kindness as a quality you'd look for in an escort, but it was vital, it turned out.

Maybe that was because it was vital in any relationship.

Kindness ought to be the foundation of anything. Of everything.

I noodled on that as I walked to my office. Along the way, my phone buzzed. I grabbed it, hoping Jake was awake.

Jake: Confession: I posed like that this morning just to get you to admit the truth.

Kate: Shameless. You are shameless.

Jake: Kidding. I was deep in the land of nod and just woke up finally. Good to know you enjoyed the view. I enjoyed all my views last night. But let's talk about tonight, Ms. Williams. I'm taking you out to dinner. I made a reservation at Momofuku, your favorite. See you at seven thirty.

I stopped walking, my heart speeding up, my smile spreading before I caught myself.

What the hell?

What was this reaction? He was suggesting a restaurant. It was one evening out.

But, no, it was a little more than that. It was how he'd heard me when I said Momofuku was my favorite.

Perhaps he'd heard me, too, when I said I liked romance.

Except our arrangement wasn't about romance. I reminded myself of that all day long as I worked. As I played with taglines and marketing slogans. As I prepped for my Sunday lunch with Trish.

Again and again, I told myself.

Even though tonight's meetup with Jake bore all the hallmarks of romance, it was not.

I needed to recalibrate to sex-only.

In the early evening, with that in mind, I sent him a message.

Kate: What is the scenario tonight?

Jake: No scenario at dinner. But once I pay the check, we're strangers who just met.

A burst of anticipation zipped through me as I read his text while walking into my kitchen. I stopped at the counter, setting a hand down and collecting myself.

But from what? From the idea of dinner or the thought of the games?

Or both?

I didn't know. In one swift move, Jake had changed the rules.

We weren't merely role-playing.

We weren't experimenting for the sake of work research.

He was taking me on a date.

And he wasn't taking no for an answer.

I didn't want to say no either.

I wanted to say yes to both.

Dating hadn't been on the weekend's agenda, but it seemed like that had changed.

I had no idea what that meant.

The not-knowing thrilled the part of me that longed for romance, a side I'd denied for some time now.

But tonight, Romantic Kate would get a chance to play.

* * *

Standing in front of my clothes, I asked the age-old question that women have asked closets for generations. "What should I wear tonight?"

As I perused a few black dresses, a couple of pretty

scoop-neck tops, and some short-sleeve blouses, I only briefly considered what Jake would like to see me in.

The thought didn't last long, and then I let it go.

That was oddly freeing—a welcome change from anxious guesses about what my date would find attractive.

But why?

As I ran my fingers down a purple top that dared to reveal just enough cleavage, I found the answer.

I wasn't dressing to impress a man.

And that wasn't because I *didn't* want to impress the man.

I did. God, did I want to impress him.

Only, I knew this man was interested in the full package—by how I felt in what I wore.

Jake wasn't the sort to be turned on by certain looks or styles. He was the kind of man turned on by the whole woman.

And that was a wildly freeing thought. A seductive one too.

Which made it incredibly dangerous as well.

But as I pulled on my favorite jeans, a sexy pair of strappy silver heels, and the purple top, I was craving the danger.

Craving the man.

Craving the whole night.

I touched up my blush and mascara, and my phone trilled—a FaceTime call. When I saw the dual images, I slid my thumb across the screen to answer the group call.

"It's Peaches and Cream. It's Frick and Frack. It's Salt

and Pepper," I said to my friends, calling me from their separate phones but patched together.

Lily arched a brow, and Nina stuck out her tongue. "Thanks so much. Glad to know you see us as twinsies," Lily said.

I shrugged saucily. "Well, you *are* calling me in tandem. And you're both in yoga pants and sports bras."

Nina rolled her eyes. "Because we're at the gym. I'm on the StairMaster, and Lily's on the elliptical one row over. And we're calling you because we like you. Or used to, I should say."

I puckered my lips and blew a kiss at them. "You still like me. You *love* me. Admit it."

"Fine, fine. We love you. Which is why we wanted to invite you out for coffee," Lily offered as her arms swept back and forth. Her phone must have been positioned on the dashboard of the machine.

"I do love coffee, but alas, I can't make it tonight."

Lily brought her face right up to the screen. "My reporter radar says you have a date."

Nina's eyes gleamed, her hair bouncing as she stepped up and up and up. "You told us we weren't allowed to set you up, and now you have a date. I'm pretty sure this means you don't love us at all."

I gulped.

Oops.

They'd both been pushing me toward Jake whenever they were given a chance. I didn't know if I wanted to tell them about this arrangement we had for the weekend. Being my best friends, they'd likely try to turn it into something more.

For a fleeting second, I wished they could.

I wished they could wave a magic wand and make it . . . *something*.

That wasn't in the cards.

But neither was lying to my friends.

I drew a breath, squared my shoulders, and spoke the truth. "It's not a date. I'm just having dinner with Jake."

Nina's face disappeared from the screen.

"What just happened?" I asked, nervous.

Lily waved a hand dismissively. "Don't worry. She just fell off the StairMaster. She'll be on the YouTube channel for Epic Gym Fumbles tonight."

I stared at my friend. "Seriously? Is she okay?"

Nina popped back up. "I'm fine, I'm fine," she said, pretending to be breathless. Then she whispered, "Just playing around. I didn't really fall. But now tell us stuff. Tell us about your *just dinner*."

"I swear it's just dinner."

As if they'd been practicing synchronized guffaws, the two of them scoffed in unison.

"Sure," Lily said.

"Right," Nina agreed.

"Guys, I mean it. He's helping me out with some work stuff. It's not a date," I said, then glanced at the time. "But I do have to go."

* * *

I headed to The Cosmopolitan, taking the escalator past The Chandelier bar, enrobed in its sheets of gorgeous crystals. As I got closer, my stomach flipped and my chest fluttered.

This felt like a date.

This felt like *romance*.

Anticipation sent sparks over my skin.

When I found Jake waiting at the restaurant bar, I paused to take in the cut of his jaw as he lifted his high-ball glass, to watch his Adam's apple bob as he knocked back a swallow. He said something to the bartender, who laughed, and I wondered what amusing thing he'd said.

My skin heated up as I watched him.

But so did my heart.

It beat faster and faster.

Insistently.

This weekend was not about companionship, pleasure, or friendship—not the paid kind, and not the kind that came in a relationship.

This weekend was about work and wallets and knowledge.

Feelings had no place in these forty-eight hours, which were more than half over.

I'd have to crush this bloom of emotion in my chest.

Jake and I were an arrangement, nothing more. And our arrangement ended after tonight.

14

KATE

My mouth watered as I read the menu.

Shishito peppers. Mushroom buns. Sautéed brussels sprouts. Kampachi.

I straightened my spine, humming happily, as I pointed to the menu. "I'll take one of everything."

Jake laughed. "That's almost always a good idea."

I arched a brow, determined to keep things fun and light tonight. "And with role-play too. Tonight, I'll order the teacher and student. Tomorrow, I'll have the handyman and housewife."

His eyes darkened a touch. "I'd like your menu, please."

I pointed to the brussels sprouts. "What's the deal with brussels sprouts?"

"You sound like a comedian about to slide into a riff," he remarked.

"Seriously though. Do you remember when brussels sprouts were the punchline of a joke? Or the horrid thing served only at school cafeterias?"

He smiled his deliciously crooked grin. Jake fit in perfectly with the restaurant's modern styling and trendy decor—put together, handsome, but not pretentious. Not showy. Simply easy on the eyes. He wore a button-down with a lightly checkered pattern and charcoal slacks. The lawyer after-hours. He looked delectable, all the more so with his unshaven jaw.

Which was all the more reason to focus on brussels sprouts.

"A punishment food," he mused. "That's what they were for a long time." He adopted a deep, patriarchal tone, shaking his finger. "Eat your brussels sprouts, Timmy, or you won't get any dessert."

I smiled. "Exactly. And now it's like they're the belle of the cooking ball. It's a competition at different restaurants to make brussels sprouts the tastiest dish in all creation."

"That is true. You can't go anywhere without brussels sprouts trying to tempt your taste buds."

"They're the vixens of vegetables. The sirens of salads."

He leaned closer. "They offer themselves up in all sorts of tantalizing forms. Sautéed, fried, roasted. How is a man or woman to resist?"

"Resistance is futile. No one can deny the power of the sprout."

Just then, despite all my lectures to myself, all that mattered was *this*. This conversation. This night. This surfeit of fun we were having. Jake was the antidote to the past several months of my life. He was the opposite of work. He was exactly how I wanted to spend my nights, and I didn't want my nights to end.

This night, of course.

We had an expiration date, since we were only spending a weekend together. And really, wasn't that all I needed? And all he wanted?

"Then don't deny it, Williams," he said, reaching across the table and gripping my hand like he was making an impassioned plea. "Don't deny the sprout."

"I won't. I can't. I shall devour them tonight." I placed my hand over my heart. "I, Kate Williams, hereby profess that I am obsessed with finding the best brussels sprouts ever."

He squeezed my hand tighter, then let go, a glint in his eyes. "I feel a bet coming on."

"Ooh. Don't get me excited." I set down the menu, eager for a wager.

He shot me a cocky smirk. "*Don't* get you excited? Are you sure about that, Williams?"

I took the bait, loving the flirting. Flirting was fine. Flirting wouldn't feed the emotions I was trying to starve out. "Fine. *Get* me excited. If you must," I said playfully.

Under the table, he slid a hand up the denim of my thigh. "If you insist," he said, his fingers traveling along my leg. He let a rumble cross his lips, then lowered his voice and murmured, "I'll bet these brussels sprouts are orgasmic."

I blinked. "That's your bet?"

He squeezed my thigh. "Yep. Nice and simple."

"And if they are?"

A smile curved his lips—no, it was more like a knowing grin. He took his time, licked his lips, then answered, "Then we do this again tomorrow."

I was quiet, saying nothing at first, letting his wager sink in.

It was almost as if Jake already knew I didn't want the weekend to end.

15

JAKE

I was surprised at the ease with which I got her to make the bet.

And at the same time, I wasn't surprised at all.

True, I'd only spent one night with her, but one night was enough to know I wanted more.

All day, I'd thought about her.

From the moment I woke up in the suite, the scent of her on the pillows, the scene of the crime still fresh—the crime being the hottest sex in my life—Kate had commandeered my thoughts.

She'd been in my head all day.

When I went to the gym with Finn and Adam, hitting the basketball courts for a pickup game.

When Finn asked how my night had been.

When I'd remarked that it was fantastic as we'd walked off the court.

"Sounds like maybe someone finally found his balls," Adam had said.

"Let me know if you need help finding yours," I'd said, the only acceptable response.

Later in the afternoon at home, I'd replayed the sex again and again.

But not only the sex. The conversation too. She'd let me in more easily than I'd thought, and I'd relished learning more about her—her past, her present, her goals.

I wanted more of that tonight.

And tomorrow too.

More Kate, before we had to shut this down.

This weekend was temporary—she had her work to focus on, and I had no interest in another Debbie situation—but there was no reason this weekend fling had to end today. Sunday night could become part of it too.

It all hinged on the veggies.

Kate arched a brow, smiling coyly at me. "You're angling for another night?"

No reason to deny the truth. We had set the boundaries, we'd mapped the exit strategy, and while I was in this, I was damn well going to be in it all the way.

I nodded, owning it. "I am. I absolutely am."

She moved a little closer, her eyes never straying from mine. "Then I hope the brussels sprouts are a ten."

I wanted to pump a fist. To kiss the air. To shout in victory because she craved the same damn thing as me.

* * *

She mimed slam-dunking a basket as we finished the appetizer. "Ten," she declared, and the sight of her like that—animated and vibrant—felt like a new detail about her, one I enjoyed knowing.

"Ten," I said, seconding her.

That felt good too—being on the same page and acknowledging it.

Setting her fork down with gusto, she shook her head in amusement, smiling. "I guess that means you'll have to take me out tomorrow night."

I feigned annoyance, then snapped my fingers. "Damn it."

We moved on to other food, chatting as we made our way through peppers and mushrooms, Kampachi and cucumbers, and a bottle of wine.

As Kate lifted her glass, she took a deep breath, as if preparing to ask something hard. "So, what's your story, Mr. Hamilton? Why are you Captain Single?"

Ah. The necessary conversation. The one I'd suspected we'd have at some point, especially since she'd opened up to me last night. But I didn't mind having it. Kate was easy to talk to—always had been.

"The truth is simple. One, my last girlfriend wanted to get serious far too quickly, and that's made me a little wary of getting involved. And two, the woman I dated before her told me when she dumped me that I was already married to work."

Kate winced. "Ouch. How did you feel about that?"

I scratched my jaw, flashing back to the breakup with Cassidy. I'd liked spending time with her, and had been starting to fall for her, but her parting comment had burned.

With good reason.

"Honestly, I felt pretty shitty at first," I admitted with a sigh. "But I knew what my goal was—to help my parents with their retirement. My dad worked his ass off while I was growing up, and the least I can do is help him enjoy his retirement now."

"That's great that you do that for them," Kate said, a softness in her voice that tugged at my heart. "I can see why it would bother you if someone you were involved with didn't understand why it was important to you."

"Exactly. My dad nearly died of a heart attack, and I have no doubt it was from working too damn hard. The least I can do is help him out."

"Oh God," she said, clasping a hand to her mouth, then letting go. "That's so tough. I'm so sorry he went through that, but I'm glad he made it." She reached out and set a hand on my arm, rubbing lightly.

I glanced down, and even though her hands had skimmed my chest last night, had roamed my body, this touch felt just as intimate as those had.

But for entirely different reasons.

Reasons I wasn't so sure I understood.

"Thanks. Me too. Obviously. That's just part of why I want to help them." My jaw clenched as I thought of all the hard times my dad went through when I was younger, and how, even as a kid, I'd wanted to do whatever I could for him. "I hated watching him and Mom struggle. When I was in middle school, I vowed I'd do whatever I could to help them. But there wasn't much I could do then."

A focused listener, she never let her eyes stray from mine. "Of course not. You were just a kid worried about

your father. But look at you—taking care of them now."
She gestured to me with a grin that felt new—one that
seemed to come from deep within. "They must be
proud of you."

A warmth like sunshine spread in my chest. She
understood why this mattered to me, why my choices
were important. "I'm proud of them. They worked hard,
they love hard, and they're enjoying their retirement as
they should. I'm lucky to have them, and I want to do
right by them and my sister. She has this kick-ass
eleven-year-old." I went on, telling her all about Carson,
our pinball passion, the basketball games, and his
sarcastic but clever style.

"He sounds like you," Kate said with a laugh that
caught me off guard. I'd heard her laugh plenty of times
before, but this one felt like it came from a different
place, a deeper place. It was softer, sweeter, and at the
same time, it seemed to say she knew me. She could
laugh at me, with me, for me.

"Yeah, he kind of is like me."

"Lucky kid," she said softly, pushing a few loose
strands of hair away from her cheek.

Instinctively, I leaned closer and took over for her,
brushing those strands out of the way, tucking them
behind her ear.

"Thank you," she said.

"No, *thank you*," I said, lingering on her hair, taking
the time to run my fingers over it. Her hair was entic-
ingly soft. "I fucking love your hair."

The compliment came out unbidden, and it was
wholly necessary. Her chestnut strands were gorgeous.

A faint blush spread on her cheeks. "And thank you for that too."

I lowered my hand, unsure of how to respond. Over the last few months, I'd become accustomed to her sass, to her fire, but this was another side of Kate I'd seen this weekend.

A softer side. A vulnerable side. Sides I dug a whole lot. Even in spite of what had happened with her ex, she seemed to open up easily, to let me in. And every time she let me see more of her, I found myself wanting to kick that door open, know her better, understand her more deeply. And let her into my world too.

Finally, I found the words. "Thanks for listening."

"I like hearing about your family. And your nephew. It's great that you're a part of his life," she said.

"He's a good kid. I love getting the chance to spend time with him. And to look out for my sister."

"This is the same sister who told you to stop working this weekend," she said, arching a brow.

"That's the one."

She took another sip, her expression amused. "Smart sister. Good idea she had."

I inched closer to Kate again, wanting to be in her orbit, wanting to be near her. Hell, maybe it was the wine. Maybe the peppers. Maybe it was just the aphrodisiac effect of a fantastic meal. But this woman was doing something to me, heating me all over. It wasn't merely with lust. It was lust mixed with something else, something new. "Best idea ever."

Lifting her glass, she offered it in a toast. "Let's drink to fantastic weekends."

I clinked back. "Like this one."

She'd just taken a drink of her wine when a voice cut across the table. A pretty, feminine voice. "Hey, girl! Don't you look gorgeous tonight?"

Kate whipped her head to look, then she grinned. "And I see you're slumming it, as always," Kate said, rolling her eyes at the other woman's just-stepped-off-a-movie-set dress.

Holy smokes. The other woman was Ivy Carmichael, one of the wealthiest people in Las Vegas.

"Seriously, that Badgley Mischka is hot," Kate continued.

"Thank you," Ivy said, smoothing a hand over her red dress, then tapping the table with a perfectly polished finger. "Did you get dessert? You have to try the rainbow cake. I'm going to have ten delivered for our next book club."

"Ten? That seems a little low. That's one cake per person," Kate said, deadpan.

The other woman tapped her lip, frowning. "True. Better make it twenty—another for everyone to take home. I better place my order now. Tuesday will be here before we know it."

"Excellent. As president of the club, I approve. But I have a confession—I didn't make it through the book. I switched to a hot new romance."

Ivy dipped her head and whispered, "Same here." Then she turned to me, and Kate jumped in.

"Ivy, this is my good friend Jake Hamilton. Jake, this is Ivy Carmichael."

I extended a hand. "Pleasure to meet you. Love your hotel."

Ivy beamed. "Thank you." She nodded toward Kate. "And I hope you're treating my book club president exceedingly well."

I grinned. "Only the best for Kate."

"That's what I like to hear," the woman who owned one of the most luxurious casinos on the Strip said to me. Then she added to Kate in a not-so-hushed whisper, eyes aimed in my direction, "*Friend.*"

Ivy shook her head, not buying it.

Smart woman. Brilliant woman.

Kate simply shrugged and smiled.

When Ivy turned to leave, a man about the size of a tree followed close behind her. Bodyguard maybe.

Ivy glanced back at the man, her eyes lingering on him.

As they left, I returned my focus to Kate. "So, you're casual friends with one of the Carmichael sisters?"

Kate shrugged impishly, her hazel eyes twinkling with mischief. I'd never noticed her eyes could be so playful—another thing about Kate Williams I filed away. The drawer of details was filling up.

"She's a voracious reader," Kate said. "Very clever and insightful. We usually meet in a private room at the Rapture, so I can't complain about that. And she has quite a sweet tooth, so it works out well."

I sensed a chance to learn more about where Kate's mind was. "Speaking of insight, she seemed to doubt you when you called me a friend . . ."

Kate licked her lips, lifted her glass, and took a sip. "Like I said, she's insightful."

For the second time that night, I wanted to punch the air.

But I also wanted something else.

I wanted a kiss.

So I took one. I leaned across the table, clasped her cheek, and dropped my lips to hers. The second we made contact, I moaned, and she murmured. Closing my eyes, I savored her lips, kissing her tenderly. We were in a classy joint, after all. Now wasn't the time to devour her mouth. And right then, I didn't want to devour. I wanted to savor the taste of the wine on her lips, the softness of her kiss. Maybe I was buzzed from the alcohol. Or possibly from the evening. Whatever it was, my mind went hazy, and Kate Williams went to my head.

Her hair and her lips, her mind and her mouth . . . From her big heart to the way she listened, her hotel friend was spot on.

Kate was not a friend.

And I didn't feel friendly at all.

She didn't seem to either, as she murmured softly, sighing when I broke the kiss.

"Insightful," she whispered.

"Very insightful," I replied, blinking to clear my head again.

A few seconds later, the waiter swung by, asking if we needed anything.

That broke the spell.

"We're all good," I told the man.

When he left, Kate jumped back to an earlier topic. "So, do you think you're married to work, like your ex said?"

I liked that she wanted to finish the conversation that had been interrupted by Ivy's appearance. It said she was focused on getting to know me.

I scrubbed a hand across the back of my neck, wanting to answer her honestly, as she'd done with me last night. "The age-old question." I'd let her go first. "Are you?"

She nodded. "Oh, definitely. But once I get this debt paid off, I want to get a massage and lie out by the pool and read, read, read. Just get lost in a book."

"One of my favorite things to do too."

"Book lovers unite," she said with a grin.

"And to answer your question," I said, "maybe I am caught up in work. But at the time, it wasn't something I planned to change."

"And now?"

I flinched. Was she asking about the weekend? Did she mean would I change for her?

Tension radiated through my bones as a familiar feeling spread over me. *Flight.* The desire to take off when a woman started encroaching on my carefully constructed goals.

But then, just as quickly as it had come, that sensation dissipated.

Maybe because that wasn't what Kate was truly asking?

Or maybe because of something else . . .

When I met her gaze, searching those hazel eyes, I saw something in them I hadn't seen in other women.

Not in Debbie. Not in Cassidy.

Something I wasn't looking for.

But now, it was something I was pretty sure I wanted.

Someone who got me.

Who understood me.

And maybe, just maybe, someone I wanted to change for.

That was what I had been realizing all night with her, what I'd been trying to figure out as we talked.

That was who she was.

The realization nearly knocked the breath out of me.

What the hell?

This was not on the agenda, not part of the weekend plan.

Catching feelings was not on the list of things to do with a woman who wanted nothing to do with emotions.

I had to get it together.

I needed to center myself and zero in on the mission of the weekend. Fantasies. Pleasure. Role-play.

Not the role-play of a great date.

Not the role-play of a fantastic conversation.

And not the role-play of starting to fall for someone.

So I did my best impression of a lawyer, evading the question as I said, "You never know."

Then I paid the bill, cleared my throat, and told her in that commanding tone she seemed to love that we'd meet at The Chandelier bar downstairs in a few minutes.

Sex.

We'd focus on sex.

And that would get my mind off the inconvenient feelings that were threatening to uproot a perfectly good weekend of hotel sex.

16

KATE

The Chandelier Bar dripped with sensuality. Crystal strands hung from the ceiling, wrapping the bar in a rich, luxurious feel.

Silver and pink, with plush stools and lounges—this was a bar for hot romance.

It spoke of trysts and arrangements. It spoke of passion and nights with your lover.

It spoke of promises.

Forever promises, in some cases.

I'd read a novel where the hero proposed to the heroine here in this bar.

As I sat perched on a stool, I replayed the scene, remembering how he'd asked the question, a smile tugging at my lips.

But then, I dismissed the scene, the memory.

Why would I be thinking of scenes like that tonight?

Jake and I were simply playing a game. We weren't having a date or a love affair.

Fine, we *might* acknowledge that more was brewing

between us than mere friendship. But we'd never pretended we were *only* friends. We'd acknowledged our mutual attraction. That didn't mean we were going to act on it beyond this weekend.

We had an expiration date—we'd simply extended it by twenty-four hours.

A late checkout, if you will.

But we still had one, and we'd adhere to it.

I wasn't keen on getting involved, and he'd made his feelings on relationships abundantly clear.

He'd said it himself when I asked the question at Edge two nights ago.

Like a date?

No. Like dinner. They serve food. You eat. It's good.

Even if we kissed, even if we touched, these were roles we were acting out.

This thing was all one giant scenario.

And I needed to get my head in the game.

I squared my shoulders, took a drink of my water— I'd had enough wine at the restaurant—and prepped to meet a stranger.

We had our parts to play.

* * *

"Is this seat taken?" His smile was crooked and full of dirty intent.

I shot him a playful look in return, tapping the stool with my burgundy fingernail. "It is now."

He parked himself on it, his eyes roaming over me, then landing on my glass. "Can I buy you a drink?"

It was a classic pickup line.

All pickup lines were.

But that was what we were playing tonight, and my skin was already tingling. Especially since this was a bar for coupling up—the duo at the end of the counter would be coupling upstairs soon, from the look of it.

The two gorgeous women in tight dresses couldn't keep their hands off each other. The dark-skinned woman in red threaded her fingers through the blonde's hair. The blonde leaned into the touch like she was luxuriating in it.

I wasn't usually turned on by two women—that wasn't my thing. But public shows of affection were my kink.

I tipped my forehead in their direction. "I'll have what they're having."

Jake's gaze followed mine, and he murmured appreciatively as he perused the two women. "Looks like they're having each other."

He rose, moved his stool closer to mine, then gestured to the bartender and pointed to the women. "We'll have what they're having."

"Two martinis, coming right up," the man said, and set to work.

Jake turned to me, his eyes eating me up. "So, are you from around here? Or just in town for the weekend?"

Time to improvise. "Passing through. I'm on my way to New York, and I stopped here for the weekend with friends."

An eyebrow rose. "A girls' weekend? Has it been good so far?"

I nibbled on the corner of my lip, shamelessly staring at him because I could. Because I fucking could. "It's getting better. A lot better," I said, taking my time to punctuate those last words with a pop of my lips, so my meaning was clear.

A groan emanated from his throat. "I'd say so too," he rasped out as his eyes slid down to my cleavage, then back up to my face.

A ribbon of heat unfurled in me, spreading through my body, pulsing between my legs. Out of the corner of my eye, the two women moved closer to each other. The woman in red took the lead, leaning in and pressing a kiss to the blonde's neck.

I went up in flames. "They're going upstairs soon," I said, unable to resist. My core ached. My desire shot sky-high. There was nothing that thrilled me more than strangers touching.

Until Jake set a hand on my thigh, and I trembled.

Oh, God.

This man.

He turned me on more.

He turned me inside out with pleasure.

Sliding his hand up my thigh, he shifted closer, his voice low and husky near my ear. "The blonde is about to be devoured. In a few minutes, she'll be on the hotel sink, skirt hiked up, panties around her ankles, legs spread."

The fire was stoked.

I shuddered, picturing that.

But I wasn't picturing *them*.

I was seeing me on that hotel sink.

Me leaning against the mirror.

Me parting my legs.

For this sexy, dirty stranger.

"They don't even know each other's names," I said.

"No names, no professions," he said, his hand gliding higher up my thigh, closer, closer still.

I swallowed roughly. My throat was dry. "Just desire," I whispered.

Under the bar, his hand traveled to my center, and he cupped me.

"Oh God," I gasped, closing my eyes, giving in briefly to the enticing sensation of his hand where I wanted him. "That's all they want. To make each other feel incredible," I whispered.

His fingers dipped between my legs, against the denim, as he stroked me, arousing me further, sending me higher.

"You know what I think would feel incredible?"

"Tell me," I said, practically panting.

He dipped his face to my neck, dusting his lips across my skin, his stubble sending sparks over me. "I'd like to take you to my room, strip you, and show you what I want to do to you with my tongue," he said, flicking the tip of it along my neck.

My vision blurred.

I was on the edge already.

My panties were damp.

My skin sizzled.

This stranger knew how to wind me up.

"I want that," I said, ready to beg for it.

He pressed a kiss to my neck as he cupped me again under the bar. "I bet you'd love spreading your legs for me. Showing me how wet you are. Letting me taste your sweetness."

This was torture. Exquisite torture. I was dying for him. "I bet you'd love devouring me. I bet you want to fuck me with your tongue," I said, giving as good as he gave.

"Fuck," he groaned.

"Here are your drinks."

I snapped out of the moment when the bartender brought our martinis.

I looked at Jake, whose eyes blazed black with desire. I had no interest in drinking. I wanted to be drunk on him. He lifted a glass, knocked some back, tossed some bills on the bar, and said, "Come with me. I need to go down on you so fucking bad right now."

* * *

In the elevator, he pushed me into a corner, his hands roaming over my chest, squeezing my breasts. "Do you have any idea how much I want to bury my face between your legs?"

"I'm getting an inkling," I said playfully.

Jake was voracious in the bedroom, but he particularly seemed to love giving oral.

I couldn't argue with that.

I'd dreamed about great oral sex.

I'd fantasized about it.

But I'd never had a man who ate me the way he did.

With absolute passion.

He'd gone down on me last night like I was dessert.

Like I was his decadent dessert, and he'd been craving me all day, all week, all year.

He kissed me like that now too. Like a man unhinged. He practically shook with lust. I swore I could smell it on him. His desire. His fervor.

It was utterly addictive.

When we got off the elevator, I didn't ask when he'd booked the room.

I didn't care.

All I cared about was getting naked for him.

Inside the room, he practically tore off my clothes. We were frenzied, fevered, stripping as we walked, leaving clothes strewn along the carpet. I yanked at his shirt, needing to see his chest, to drag my nails along the grooves of his abs.

He tugged at my jeans, unzipping them as we rushed to enact the scene we'd already mapped out.

When we reached the bathroom, I kicked off my heels, and in seconds flat, he'd pulled my jeans to my ankles, helping me step out of them.

He grunted, as if consumed with getting me naked.

I wanted to be consumed by him.

By his need.

By his intensity.

By his utter carnality.

When I was down to only panties, he tugged them off so quickly they still dangled on my right leg, and he didn't care. He lifted me onto the sink, spread my legs, and kissed my pussy.

I saw stars.

I cried out from that first touch, that first lick.

He was on fire.

I stared down at him, his dark hair in my hands, his mouth on my wetness, his palms on my thighs.

He kissed and sucked and groaned.

Jake Hamilton might be pretending to be a stranger. But I knew what he was. It was so crystal clear.

Jake was an animal.

And I loved his hunger.

I adored his appetite.

I craved his ravenous need for me.

His hands curled around my legs as my undies finally slipped off. Naked, I scooted back on the vanity, my spine against the mirror, my fingers roped in his hair. He didn't break contact with my pussy. His miraculous tongue was on a mission to please me, taunt me, fuck me.

My God, that was what he did with his tongue.

He fucked.

I was in dirty heaven. As I stared at him, watching him, sparks racing over my skin, lust coiling in my body, I saw myself.

I hadn't noticed the other mirror in the bathroom at first. But there it was—across from the sink, reflecting me back to me.

Or, I should say, *us*.

What I saw made the temperature in me shoot up ten thousand degrees. A wanton woman, hair in a tumble, legs spread wide. A commanding man, bent down, face buried between her thighs. Pleasure radiated across my skin, evident in my face.

I'd rarely watched myself before.

I'd often watched others, and then only the start of their trysts.

But now I was watching two people pretending to be strangers. Two people utterly lost in the moment. Two people wanting.

Wanting so badly what the other had to give.

He wanted to give me the highest high.

And I wanted to take it.

Oh God, did I ever want to take it. My hands curled around his skull, and I tried to watch as he sucked harder on my clit, as his tongue stroked inside me, as his strong hands gripped my ass mercilessly.

But as the pleasure swirled in me, I couldn't keep my eyes open. I couldn't focus.

I could only feel.

I felt the utter intensity of his desire.

I felt my own, as ecstasy ran roughshod over my body, and I broke.

Shattering.

Crying out.

Saying his name.

Chanting it.

Because no matter how well we played, no matter how far we went, he wasn't a stranger.

He was my weekend lover, and I didn't want the weekend to end.

* * *

He shed his pants and boxers, and we moved to the bed, where he set me down on my side. "Need to be inside you, Kate. Need it now," he gritted out.

We weren't strangers at all.

Had we ever been tonight? Or had we always been us, just amped up? That was what I was learning about role-playing. Pretending you were someone else only made sex with your lover hotter. It deepened the intimacy. It deepened the connection.

And I wanted that tonight. I wanted him in every way.

"Have me, Jake," I said, the most natural words I'd ever spoken.

Then I said something else. Something I wanted. I met his gaze, swallowed, and spoke. "I'm on protection. And I'm clean."

He moaned. "I'm clean too. I've been tested."

That was all he needed to say.

He kneeled between my legs, one knee on each side of my outstretched leg, then he lifted my right leg up on his shoulder.

"The pretzel," I said with a light laugh.

"Be my pretzel, Kate," he said playfully. His expression darkened, became more intense as he rubbed the head of his cock against all the wetness between my legs —wetness he was responsible for. "This position should let you feel me nice and deep like you're on all fours, but I can look at you, so it's more intimate."

That word seemed to roll around on his tongue.

Intimate.

Like he coveted intimacy. Like he ached for it.

And I did too.

I wanted more than role-play.

More than a game.

I wanted intimacy, and I wanted Jake to have me like this.

The way he wanted it.

He thrust into me, sliding deep, filling me. My mouth fell open, my lips parted, and the sounds I made were obscene—groans and grunts and sexy sighs.

Pleasure rippled through my body as he sank into me.

As he filled me completely.

And as he looked at me, there was lust in his gaze, but something else too.

Something I hadn't seen before in him.

Maybe because I hadn't been looking.

Or maybe because last night we didn't look at each other.

Now we did, and as he kneeled between my legs, rocking, swiveling, thrusting, I saw need.

And want.

And *more.*

I saw an insatiable desire for more.

Was it more sex he wanted?

Or more nights like this?

Nights where we talked, where we played, where we fucked.

I wanted to know, but I also wanted to give in completely.

That was easy because he was in charge. He was in control. He was a man who liked to set the pace, to command the scene, and to have his woman.

As he fucked harder, faster, deeper, I felt like *his* woman.

And he was having me.

Dear God, he was having me, taking me, driving into me.

"Play with your tits, baby. I want to watch you touch yourself," he ordered.

And I was all too happy to have something to do with my hands. I reached for my breasts, cupping, kneading.

He groaned as he watched me, his hands curled around my hips as he pumped. "So fucking sexy. So fucking hot. I get off to that image."

"You do? You have?"

"Yes, so many times. You're so damn sexy. So damn beautiful," he murmured, never stopping.

My skin tingled, and my body was bathed in pleasure. Every cell sang in bliss. Every inch of me longed for that exquisite release.

My eyes floated closed, but once they did, he growled. "Watch me. Watch me fuck you till you come so damn hard."

I opened my eyes, nodding, wanting the same thing. "I want to look at you when you come too. Want to see your face."

I played with my breasts, fondling myself, then I let go of one, slid my hand between my legs, and stroked my clit.

My hips shot up. My lips parted. I was at the edge, ready to fly.

"Yes, come for me," he urged. "Come so fucking hard for me."

He didn't have to ask twice. I was already there, bucking and writhing and losing my hold on reality.

The world blurred, spiraling away into neon bliss, into electric ecstasy. I squeezed my eyes shut, my climax taking over, pummeling me with waves of lust, of pleasure.

He groaned, his sounds growing louder, more erratic. His body jerked, and I wanted to see his face. I wanted to watch him hit that place I'd been.

Opening my eyes, I discovered the sexiest sight ever.

Jake's handsome features tight with pleasure as he reached his release, calling out my name. He let go at last.

Falling onto me. Clasping me. Holding me tight.

Somewhere in the back of my mind, I knew I should leave.

I knew this was risky.

If I stayed, I'd want more than Sunday.

I'd want Monday, Tuesday, Wednesday.

I'd want every day.

That was the problem.

I was becoming addicted to this man.

And I had to find a way to break my addiction.

It wouldn't be tonight though.

And it wouldn't be in the morning either, because I woke up to him curled around me again. To his hard shaft against my back. To his kisses on my neck. And like that, I led him back into me. I guided his erection between my legs, rubbing him against me, where I was ready for him.

We had sleepy early morning sex. Slow and tender.

We took our time.

There was no pounding.

No driving.

Only us, tangled together under the sheets, and it felt dangerously like all the things it wasn't supposed to be.

17

KATE

That feeling you got when you've done something you shouldn't?

It hit me as the sun cast its rays through the window, illuminating the messy bed, the sprawl of sheets, the sleeping man next to me.

I took a deep, fulfilling breath. I hadn't felt this good in ages. Maybe I'd see if he wanted to order breakfast or grab a bite at the Egg Slut downstairs. We could order coffee, make our evening plans, then say goodbye for the day.

We were good at this—spending time together.

Satisfied with that plan, I let my eyes roam over him, practically whistling a happy tune. We must have fallen back to sleep after our nookie at the crack of dawn. It was probably nine. Plenty of time to make my meeting.

I glanced at the clock.

Wait. Was that right?

I squinted.

It was eleven in the morning?

I blinked. Checked again.

And the clock still mocked me with its red digital numbers telling me I'd slept far too late.

I sat bolt upright.

Trish.

I had lunch with Trish in an hour. My heart skittered with panic. I had nothing to wear, my home was twenty minutes away if I was lucky, and even if I wore yesterday's clothes, I didn't have clean panties. The ones I wore last night were useless.

Grabbing my phone from the nightstand, I checked my texts, praying that she'd changed her mind about a check-in meeting.

No such luck.

The text from her was the opposite.

Trish: Hi, Kate! Can you meet a touch early? I have an appointment at one, so if we could meet a few minutes ahead of time, that would be great.

I let out a long stream of muttered curses, my frustration bubbling over.

"What's wrong?"

I swung my gaze to Jake, who yawned, rubbing his eyes.

I dragged a hand through my messy hair. "I have to meet my boss in forty-five minutes, and I have nothing to wear that doesn't scream *walk of shame.*"

He blinked. "Let's go downstairs and go shopping for you."

I sliced that notion off at the knees. I didn't need his help. Jumping out of bed, I hunted for my clothes, finding them in a trail across the carpet. "This is my problem. I need to solve it," I said as I pulled on my useless underwear. "Besides, it's quicker and easier on my own."

"But I can—"

His phone buzzed. He grabbed it, groaning as he read the text. "It's Carson. I told him I'd go to his soccer match. Evidently, sex makes me stupid too. I need to run." He scrambled out of bed, pulled on his slacks, and tugged me in for a kiss after I jerked my top over my head.

A boyfriend kiss.

One that said *I'll see you later.*

Then he left.

Out of bed in one-minute flat.

I didn't dwell on his swift departure as I grabbed the room key, hustled to the elevator, and darted to The Cosmopolitan's shops to buy new panties and a basic black top. Then, after rushing back to the elevator, I zipped up to the room for a shower.

What pissed me off wasn't Jake or how he'd left.

It was me.

I'd messed up.

I'd forgotten.

I'd gotten swept up in a whirlwind of sex and conversation and closeness. I'd been caught up in what felt like dating, getting to know him, getting to like him.

I soaped my body, scrubbing harder, trying to wash off the dirty.

This was supposed to be a weekend of research, not of lolling like a pussycat in the sun, licking my fur and purring.

And it was definitely not meant to be a weekend of feelings.

Of falling.

Of sliding into romance with a man who was clever, charming, a beast in bed . . . and a gentleman outside of it.

My heart stuttered as I thought about our talk last night.

Thought about the way he'd kissed me at the table.

And thought, too, of the intensity with which he'd taken me.

He was relentless, and relentlessly obsessed with making me feel good.

Yet, the morning after, I felt dirty, like I'd done something wrong by seeking real-world experience.

Like I should have relied on brains and research rather than using the excuse to scratch an itch.

And perhaps I should have.

I knew better—no scratching itches when they interfered with my focus.

Hopping out of the shower, I towel-dried my hair, twisted it in a bun, swiped on some gloss and powder from my purse, and pulled on my new panties.

Once I dressed, I marched out of the room, not even glancing at the carnage of the night.

I didn't have time for romance.

I clearly didn't have time for sex.

I hightailed it to the Bellagio, meeting Trish a few minutes late at her favorite Asian restaurant.

"Tell me what you've got," she said with a grin.

I flashed back on the weekend.

Don't you deserve this?

Every woman should feel spectacular.

Indulge your senses.

But as I shared my marketing thoughts, I didn't feel spectacular. I didn't feel like I deserved anything.

I felt dirty rather than decadent.

Especially since I was falling for a man who didn't want strings.

Sort of like falling for an escort, only infinitely more foolish.

* * *

When I left the meeting, I texted Jake to tell him that I was busy the rest of the day and couldn't meet him that night.

His reply told me everything I needed to know.

18

JAKE

"Yes!"

I thrust my arms up in a V for victory as Carson scored a goal for the Cougars.

"Way to go!" my sister yelled, louder and prouder, at least by a little bit.

We high-fived each other as her kid fist-bumped his teammates by the net.

"He's the man," I said to Christine when the action in the game resumed.

"And so are you. Thank you for showing up. It's really good to have you here." She rested her head briefly on my shoulder. "For him and for me."

I tousled her hair. "Good to be here. It's not a chore. I love it—and you."

"Ditto," she said.

This was an excellent Sunday. Morning sex, family bonding, and my nephew owning the soccer field.

I couldn't complain—not one bit.

Well, I could.

Kate had seemed slightly out of sorts when I took off this morning.

But we'd both overslept, and she didn't have the luxury of living as close to the hotel as I did. I'd grabbed a quick shower, pulled on jeans and a T-shirt, and still reached the game on time. I should check in with her soon, see if she made it to her meeting, and then make some plans with her for tonight.

As Carson's team moved downfield, I shouted, "Keep it up, Cougs!"

Christine shot me a glance. "You're in a festive mood."

"And why shouldn't I be?"

She lifted a curious brow. "Why *should* you be? Does this mean you took my advice for the weekend?"

I held out my right hand as if showing off a manicure. "Yes, I went to the spa. Had my nails done." I dragged a hand down my cheek. "Indulged in a facial. And then got a hot-stone massage."

She rolled her eyes. "Smart-ass."

"Learned it from you," I said. Then, because I was in a good mood, I tossed her a crumb of gossip. "I took the weekend off. Spent some time with Kate."

She gasped, her hand flying to her mouth.

"Excited much?" I teased. "Also, *why* are you excited so much?"

She dropped her hand by her side, nearly squealing, and my sister is not a squealer. "Like I said, you sparkle around her."

I shook my head, but I was laughing as I denied it. "I'm not a sparkler."

"So, how was it?"

I pretended to be offended. "I don't sparkle and tell."

Her arm darted out, and she swatted my shoulder. "So, you did?"

Ah, hell.

My sister was such a sneak. I hadn't meant to give away the personal details.

But then again, I was in a good mood, and good moods could loosen lips. I gave a *what can I say* shrug. "We spent some time together, and it was nice."

"Nice? It was *nice*? Waiters are nice. A penguin back-pack is nice. A thank-you card is nice. A night or two with the woman you've had it bad for is not nice. It's either fantastic or something you never want to repeat." She parked her hands on her hips. "Which one was it?"

As Christine glared at me, I made my decision. It was official. My sister was a mind reader, no two ways about it.

"Kate is great," I said, trying to rein in a grin.

She pumped a fist. "Knew it. Called it. When do you see her again?"

"Tonight, as a matter of fact." As I said it, I made another decision too.

Tonight, I'd let Kate know.

I'd make it clear I wanted more than a simple exten-sion to our weekend.

I wanted to see what might happen beyond the boundaries of our deal.

Because I'd realized last night that when we were together, wrapped up in each other, I hadn't wanted to let her go. It wasn't just the earth-shattering sex. It was her. I wanted to learn more about her. To talk over shishito peppers and wine, to discuss books and friends, to chat about life and this city and what makes us tick.

That was what we had done this weekend.

We'd   hadn't   merely   slept   together. We'd *been* together.

My sister was right. My friends were right. There was something between Kate and me, and it was time to explore it fully.

And it was time I admitted it to Kate, whether or not she was ready for more than an arrangement. Was she? I didn't know. But maybe her feelings had changed this weekend too.

I grabbed my phone to text her, just as a message from her popped up.

Kate: I'm slammed tonight. Sorry! I guess I'll lose this bet. But this weekend was fun! Thanks again.

I blinked, the hair on my neck standing on end.

Was my phone infected? Had I been hacked? Was this a bug?

Because what the hell?

This sure seemed like a brush-off note.

I stepped away from the field, pacing toward the parking lot, and read her text again, as if I could decipher it differently the second time around.

But on the third and fourth times, it still said the same damn thing.

She was done.

She didn't want anything more, or even another time.

Only I did.

Part of me wanted to fight. To ask what the hell had happened. But then I remembered what she'd said less than forty-eight hours ago. *One weekend, no strings, no promises, nothing more.*

She hadn't lied, never led me astray. She'd been up-front from the get-go.

The weekend was over.

And there were most definitely no strings attached for her.

I might want to give this thing a shot, but she clearly didn't.

Here was where I had to tread carefully. We had friends in common, work in common, life in common, and the woman had encountered enough jerks in her dating life.

I didn't need to be the next one.

As I walked back to the field, ready to focus on Carson and the game, I hit reply.

Jake: You are most welcome.

19

KATE

That night, I set an overabundance of alarms.

My phone. My old clock radio. And Lily.

She was an early bird, so I called to ask for help. "Hi. Any chance you can give me a good old-fashioned wake-up call tomorrow morning, so I don't miss my meeting with the potential client?"

"Like my parents asked me to do when they were in Hawaii a few weeks ago?"

"They did?" I trudged into my bedroom, making sure I had my outfit for tomorrow's pitch laid out and ready. But I was missing a belt, so I headed for my bureau.

"Yes, they said the hotel had forgotten their wake-up call for a sunrise boat trip with the dolphins, and they missed that, and they didn't want to miss their flight home, so they asked me to call them."

"And you did?"

"Yes, but I also used it as an opportunity to lovingly guide them into the twenty-first century with a reminder that no one uses hotel wake-up calls anymore, since we all have cell phones."

"Oh," I said half-heartedly as I found the belt I wanted to wear.

"Hello! Earth to Kate?"

"What?" I looked up from the accessory in the sock drawer.

"Are you listening to me?"

"Yes. Your parents are old, and you think I am too."

"Kate," she said softly. "That's not my point. It's this —you're not yourself. Of course I'm happy to give you a wake-up call, though it *is* the twenty-first century and your phone alert will work. But you're so listless right now. And that's so not you. Last time we talked, you were cheery and sassy and heading out to meet Jake. Now you're like . . . well, you're like someone who missed a sunrise boat trip with dolphins."

I forced out a laugh and tried to give myself a pep talk. "I'm good. I swear. I just need to focus on this meeting tomorrow. It's so important. If I don't win this client, it might take a few more months to get out of debt. I promise I'll be more chipper tomorrow."

We exchanged a few more niceties, then said good-bye. After I hung up, I headed into the bathroom. "Get your act together," I told my reflection.

Then I started giving myself orders.

Stop thinking about Jake.

Kick unholy ass tomorrow at work.

And don't get distracted again.

It worked.

I didn't think of Jake for a whole minute.

When I got into bed, I buried my face in the pillow, stupidly wishing he were next to me.

But what would be the point of that?

He wasn't into feelings.

He wasn't into possibilities.

And I wasn't supposed to be either.

The next day I woke early, before the alarms, and hit the gym. Logging four miles on the treadmill before seven a.m., I felt energized. I was full of endorphins and ready to tackle the pitch.

As I left, I took a long swig from my water bottle and nearly bumped into Nina. Adam followed behind her.

"Hey, you!" she said with a smile.

"Hey," I said, making my best attempt at an early morning grin.

"How was your weekend?" she asked with a wiggle of her brows.

"Yeah, how was your weekend?" Adam chimed in. "Did Jake finally ask you out? Because he won't tell me, and I've been telling him to do it for months."

Nina elbowed him with a "*Shush.*"

I frowned and turned to Adam, curious. "You've been telling him to ask me out? Care to elaborate?"

"Yeah. We know he's into you. We told him to do something about it already."

Nina snapped her gaze to her fiancé, shaking her head. "Who are you? You can't just ambush a woman with something like that."

Adam shrugged. "Just trying to move things along."

I gave them both my best smile. It wouldn't serve me to get waylaid by the Jake thought train again. "Thank you, but I'm pretty sure neither Jake nor I need anyone to move things along. We're both good with where we're at."

Nina stared daggers at her fiancé, then turned to me. "Forgive Adam. He hasn't had coffee yet. Anyway, are you ready for your pitch? You're going to do great. I'm rooting for you. Girls' night out marketing for the win," she said.

"I'm ready," I said, then glanced at my phone. "And I should go."

Nina tugged me in for a quick hug, whispering, "Don't read anything into it."

"I wasn't going to. I meant everything I said. Jake and I are on the same page. It's all good," I said with my best *I've got it together* smile.

Then I said goodbye, doing my damnedest to believe my own lies.

* * *

There were times when you had to set all the foolish emotions in your heart aside and get down to business.

This was one of them.

As Trish and I strode into the conference room she'd booked for the Sin City Escorts pitch, I held my chin high, shoved this weekend into a lockbox, then threw away the key.

Trish introduced me to Daisy DoLittle, a petite

redhead with a constellation of freckles across her nose. She didn't look like a woman who owned an escort company. She looked like she ran a ranch of abandoned hound dogs looking for a second chance.

But looks weren't everything.

I said hello, then began the presentation, all business as I made the pitch.

I zeroed in on my taglines, I shared how we could use them, and I showcased my plans to make this service a must-have gift for women to give their friends. Daisy kept an impassive face throughout, but her green eyes flickered when I shared the anecdote about the bride and her maid of honor.

"'You deserve this,' the bride told her friend," I recounted. "And that got me to thinking—honestly, don't we all deserve pleasure? Don't we all deserve to feel amazing? Don't we all deserve to explore our fantasies? That's what Sin City Escorts can do. That's what role-playing makes possible. We all become adventurers exploring the delicious land of fantasies."

A grin seemed to tug at Daisy's lips then, telling me I'd hit the right note.

When I was through, she peppered me with questions, and I answered them all.

"And what do you propose we call this new offering?" She folded her hands, waiting for my final answer.

A reel of this past weekend flickered before my eyes.

Feelings, sensations rushed over me. A tingle raced down my spine, and I recalled how Jake had made me feel.

I'd been reluctant to voice it with Trish yesterday.

And perhaps I'd been reluctant to admit it to myself, but I *knew*.

"I'd call it the Decadent Gift. Because that's what it is."

Daisy's lips curved into a satisfied grin.

A few minutes later, she declared we'd won the account.

* * *

In the back of Trish's limo, my boss recounted every second of the meeting in a play-by-play recap.

"And when you brought out that name—perfection. This is a most decadent gift."

"It is," I said.

I wished I felt half as good as I made the service sound.

But the truth was ugly.

I didn't feel decadent anymore.

I didn't feel pleased.

And I definitely wasn't happy.

All I felt was a crushing wave of relief when Trish issued me my bonus check in advance and I deposited it in the bank, then made the final payment on my debt.

But I wished that I felt something else entirely.

20

JAKE

Monday did what Mondays do.

Smack you upside the face with the reminder that it wasn't Friday, it wasn't Saturday, and it wasn't Sunday.

Monday had a particular stench to it, and it deserved it.

When my computer whirred to life that morning, it reminded me of all that I'd avoided that weekend.

Emails.

Contracts.

Clients.

I sighed heavily.

But I was there. I'd shown up. And this stuff . . . this was reliable.

My law practice was dependable.

For a flash of a second, I heard my sister's warnings about my dad, how hard he'd worked, how he'd given too much of himself to a business that was no stand-in for his family.

But that wasn't my issue.

I'd taken the weekend off and proved I wasn't married to work.

And today, I'd simply tackle my to-do list, see my nephew, and finish *Educated*.

There. I was standing in good stead.

Maybe Monday didn't have a stench after all. Maybe it was all about perspective.

As I powered through calls and emails, I patted myself on the back for the perspective I'd gained over the weekend and counted myself lucky to return to the faithful old land of contracts.

Because falling for a woman was 100 percent not reliable. In fact, I'd bet women were far worse for your heart than work.

* * *

At the basketball court the next evening, I destroyed Adam and Finn.

It was wholly satisfying.

Especially since I was playing one against two.

But not quite as satisfying as the last time I'd crushed them.

Hmm.

That was odd.

But there was no point analyzing why.

As we took off, Adam clapped me on the back. "So, it's come to my attention that I might have put my foot in my mouth yesterday morning."

I shot him a curious glance. "So, just a regular day for you?"

But he didn't laugh. He scrubbed a hand across his jaw. "It's possible I might have said something to Kate at the gym. About you."

I stopped walking, setting a hand on the concrete wall at the edge of the court. "What did you say?"

"I asked her if you'd finally found the cojones to ask her out."

I scoffed. "Why would you do that? Are you a match-maker now?"

Adam lifted his chin, owning it. "Because, dude. All you've done lately is work."

Finn cleared his throat. "And it's clear you're into her. But you get all wrapped up in the job. Don't you remember what you said to me a few years ago when I went through the same thing?"

"Yes," I grumbled, my recollection of dragging Finn's ass away from his desk after midnight crystal clear. "But I'm not as bad as you. I'm not working at two in the morning and living off energy drinks."

Finn rolled his eyes. "Give it time, my friend. You're on the road to that. And when I was obsessed with work and miserable as hell, you told me to get my act together."

"I'm not miserable," I insisted.

"But you'd be happier if you were with Kate," Adam said.

I pointed from Adam to Finn. "Are you two in cahoots with Christine? Because my sister said the same thing, and you all sound dangerously like a match-making service."

"Your sister is smart," Finn added. "And so are we. We're looking out for you."

I heaved a sigh, conceding their points, but only by a small amount. "I hear you. I appreciate that you're looking out for me. But I'm fine. I've got it together. And as shocking as this may be to believe, Kate isn't into your good friend Jake," I said. It was a helluva lot easier to admit the sorry truth when talking about myself in the third person.

"Probably because you're so ugly," Finn said.

"Definitely. She's not into ugly dudes who work too much," Adam added.

I flipped them both the bird. But curiosity about what went down with the Kate convo won out, and I took the bait. "So, what did Kate say?"

"That you guys were on the same page," Adam said.

Frowning, I scrubbed a hand across the back of my neck.

Same page?

Were we on the same page?

Was that the *thanks and you're welcome* page?

The *it's been fun* page?

The no-strings page?

Then it hit me—maybe that was the same page. But maybe we were both on the wrong page.

Because why the hell would she think I was on any other page? I hadn't told her. I hadn't said I was interested in her strings.

I'd simply said *you're welcome.*

And I was pretty sure that wasn't what you said to a woman you wanted to spend your weeknights and weekends with.

I was pretty sure, too, that it wasn't what you said to the woman who'd made you realize you could enjoy *not working.*

That you would survive being out of the office.

Because spending a weekend with someone I cared deeply for was a whole lot better.

All this time, I'd thought I needed to make the horse go faster to help my parents. To give them everything they didn't have when we were kids. But that wasn't the lesson to learn from my parents. The lesson was—find a way to be happy. Find a way to balance your life.

I took care of my parents just fine, thanks to the success of my law firm.

It was time to start taking care of my ticker too.

And saying *you're welcome* wasn't the way to do it.

That wasn't what you said to a woman you'd spent the weekend in bed with. A weekend where so much more than role-playing had been on the agenda. Where conversations and meals, nights out and nights in, sleepovers and sex without role-playing had been on the agenda.

I parked a hand on Adam's shoulder. "Your foot looks great in your mouth."

"Thanks. I think," he said, furrowing his brow.

"It reminds me of what I need to do. But I need a favor from you."

"Name it."

I told him what I needed, then I headed to my car, focused on my mission.

What exactly should I say to the woman I wanted? That was the question, and I wanted the answer.

Because I had some strings to attach.

21

KATE

The next day, I waited for The Moment.

For the heavens to part and the angels to sing.

I waited for the complete and utter bliss of being debt-free.

I was no longer paying for my ex. I was no longer responsible for my romantic mistakes.

Surely a mariachi band would serenade me at lunch.

A singing telegram would arrive and tap-dance through the afternoon lull.

None of that happened.

Work was work.

I had a satisfying job I enjoyed doing from nine to five, and I was glad to be free and clear.

But as I finished a call with Daisy about the next steps in the marketing plan for Sin City Escorts, I felt oddly empty.

Because I missed Jake.

When I said goodbye to Daisy, I glanced at the calendar and spotted a sticky note that said BOOK CLUB.

Tonight.

That would fulfill me, surely.

But wait . . .

Ivy had confessed she'd switched to reading a hot romance novel. Truth was, we never stuck to the books we chose, and our meetings ran off on tangents about the sexy books we'd devoured. I couldn't handle that tonight. Not when the missing was so fresh.

Grabbing my phone, I found the group chat with the book club gals and fired off a quick note.

Something came up, and I can't make it tonight. Keep the pages turning for me.

Then I breathed a sigh of relief.

Relief from the dread of talking about hot novels, but not from the spot inside that satisfaction and gladness and success couldn't fill.

I had to fill this emptiness somehow and soon.

Maybe I'd go for a walk and do some window-shopping, or maybe I'd work out.

I gathered my bag and got ready to take off.

Then Trish knocked on my door.

22

TRISH

Youth. It was wasted on the young.

If I'd known at age thirty what I knew more than ten years later—well, I'd be richer.

But so it goes.

Life was for the learning and the loving.

That was where I came in today.

Kate was my top employee, a vice president at my firm. And she'd been in a funk since Sunday at our lunch.

Oh, sure, she thought she was expert at covering it up. She'd flash a smile, pump a fist, give an appropriate response when I asked how she was.

But with my forty-plus years came twenty-twenty hindsight. Something was amiss, and I had a hunch what it was.

"Kate . . ." I spoke as if she were my younger sister—that was how I thought of her. "I'd expected you to be bouncing off the walls in excitement."

Her brow knit, then she quickly unknit it. "Of course. I'm thrilled about Sin City Escorts."

I shook my head. "No. I meant paying off the debt."

She swallowed, trying to school her expression. "Excuse me?"

I smiled sympathetically. "I've heard some of your conversations with the banks."

"You have?" Guilt shadowed her face as she ducked her chin.

I waved a hand airily. "Don't feel bad. It happens to many people. I'm just glad you're able to move on." I took a beat, then confirmed, "Were you able to move on?"

She nodded. "Yes, the bonus helped. Thank you, Trish."

I strode across her office and sat in the chair across from her. "I'm glad you put the money to good use. I could tell you were anxious to get it paid off."

Kate chewed on the corner of her lip for a moment, perhaps putting two and two together. "Did you offer me bonuses so that I could pay it off sooner?"

With an impish grin, I shrugged. "I didn't give you anything you didn't deserve."

"Trish," she said softly. "You didn't have to."

I swung my high-heeled foot back and forth. "Kate, I don't do anything because I have to. I do things because I want to. And now I *want* to give you a piece of advice."

"Okay," she said with a tentative laugh.

I drew a steadying breath. "I have a hunch this little funk you're in . . ." I gestured to the space around her to illustrate the cloud of annoyance that followed her like a perfume. "You could resolve it easily."

"What do you mean?"

But of course, she had no idea I knew what she'd been up to this weekend.

Nor did I ever want her to know that I'd played a part.

But I had. At times, I'd arranged and nudged and acted as a fairy godmother. And a fairy had to do what a fairy had to do.

The lovely little secret of Las Vegas was *this*—powerful women populated the city in strategic places, and we all played our part in making dreams come true, sometimes for ourselves and sometimes for others.

Some people believed this city was a man's world, and in many ways, Vegas still was.

But in other respects, this city catered to women. It was run by women. Women were rising up.

If I were the type to call it "girl power," well, I'd say it. But I didn't believe women should be called girls. I did believe in woman power though.

That was why I'd ensured Kate had opportunities to earn her way out of her money troubles sooner rather than later.

That was the extent of my role—well, along with my ever-so-subtle suggestion that she bring a friend along on her observation adventure. As her employer, I couldn't very well tell her to shag a man.

But I had powerful friends willing to help me help Kate. Friends who knew that Kate had her eye on someone. Other friends had helped too—some more than others—but some secrets couldn't be revealed.

Yes, I used my network to my advantage. Not sorry.

But now Kate was in a funk again. I didn't want her to think she *had* to be with a man. I was perfectly content being single. I didn't need a man or a woman to complete me. But she was clearly miserable without this *particular* man, which called for my intervention. Perhaps my stubborn vice president needed a gentle kick from my Louboutins.

"Kate," I said in a brook-no-nonsense tone, "it occurred to me that a woman who accomplished two major goals yesterday shouldn't give up on what she wants from a certain *friend* without a fight." I rose and smoothed my skirt with a flick, giving her an encouraging but implacable smile. "Now, why don't you think of that while you go and sort out your plan of action?"

Then I walked out, leaving her with something to chew on.

Life advice. How I loved giving it.

23

KATE

Two things were official.

I had the coolest boss ever.

And I . . . I was a stubborn mule.

Wait. There was a third thing. I wanted my *friend.* I wanted to see what Jake and I might become given more than a weekend.

Was I in love with him?

I was falling in that direction.

But the last time I'd fallen for someone, I'd been burned, badly. I'd trusted someone who'd used me and left me at financial and emotional rock bottom.

I hadn't suspected a thing, and that scared the hell out of me. If I'd been fooled once . . .

The scars of betrayal had turned me off of love. Made me shut it out.

But those scars were temporary, as it turned out. I'd worked hard to clear the way to move on. I was free, and I needed to act like it, not shut myself off in fear.

Life came without guarantees. There were people

like Damon out there, good at romance and deception. But just because Damon had screwed me over didn't mean Jake would.

Emotions were a gamble, but I didn't want to miss out on a chance at love because I cinched my protective armor too tight.

The weekend with Jake had been incredible, and it wasn't simply the sex.

It was the way we connected.

It was the ease of our conversations.

It was the tenderness in his touch.

And the roughness too.

It was everything.

I trusted him with my fantasies because . . . well, because I trusted him.

And it was time to trust myself again too.

I didn't know if Jake would want to give us a shot, but I'd never know if I didn't try.

To sort this out, though, I needed my friends.

I needed Lily and Nina, and I knew where they'd be.

At book club.

Decided and almost optimistic, I grabbed my purse, slung it over my shoulder, and didn't delay any longer than it took to pop into Trish's office to thank her. Then I fired off a note to my best friends as I made my way out of the office, letting them know to expect me after all.

Kate: I need your help, you two. This is a major mayday.

Nina: We are here for you!

Lily: Get your cute ass over to The Extravagant lobby now!

The hotel wasn't far from my office, so I marched down the Strip, passing the fountains at the Bellagio.

Funny, how just a few nights ago those fountains had framed my thoughts about Jake. As I walked past them now, watching them dance in the air, their patterns underscored a new mind-set. A new plan.

A plan that said *Why wait?*

When I reached The Extravagant, my two closest friends were waiting for me.

We huddled in a corner, and I let the truth out. "It was more than dinner with Jake this weekend. We spent the whole time together, and I'm definitely falling for him. I want to see where it goes."

Nina cooed.

Lily clapped.

I looked between them, grateful for their encouragement, but hoping for something more tactical. "So . . . what do I do?"

"Tell him," Nina insisted.

"Take a chance," Lily added. "I promise—accouterments are worth it."

We all laughed. "Jake is more than an accouterment," I said. It gave me a thrill to hear myself say that aloud.

Now I had to take the chance.

It was that simple.

It was always that simple.

I just had to trust myself enough to do it.

With a deep breath, I tapped out a text to the man who'd captured my body, my mind, and my heart.

Kate: Let's make a bet. Ready? I bet I was wildly wrong on Sunday when I canceled our evening by text. I bet I feel incredibly foolish for giving up a chance to see you again. I bet I'd like another shot at another night. Then another. Then another.

The stakes are simple: you and me.

Let me know if you want to take this bet.

Xoxo

Kate

Perhaps the heavens had parted after all.

As Lily, Nina, and I walked over to the Rapture, I told myself to be patient. He'd respond when he was ready.

But when I reached the club, he was already there, waiting outside.

24

JAKE

Kate was not the only one who paid attention.

I listened to details and filed them away—especially details about Kate.

Like on Saturday night, when Ivy had stopped at our table and in the course of conversation had mentioned the date of the book club.

That was how I knew she'd be here. I'd simply confirmed the time with Nina, via Adam.

Because I wanted to show up for Kate.

I wanted her to know I'd listened.

And I wanted her to know I recognized when I'd messed up, and I could admit it and try to fix it.

The second she stepped into view, I drank her in— sexy as sin in tight jeans, heels, and a dark-gray top, her chestnut hair loose and curling over her shoulders in waves.

My God, she was beautiful.

And smart.

And fiery.

And kind too.

She was exactly the woman I wanted to spend my nights with.

And she deserved more than a *you're welcome*.

I closed the distance between us and stopped in front of her. Her friends kept walking, waving goodbye like they had a secret.

"What are you doing here?" Kate asked, confusion knitting her brow. "I just sent my text about three minutes ago."

"I haven't checked my phone. I'm here because I wanted to tell you something." I was ready to lay my heart on the line.

"I want to tell you something too."

Torn between taking the lead and being a gentleman, I chose both. "Ladies first, but you should know I'm here about a new role I want to play."

She cocked her head, looking intrigued. "Oh. What is it?"

I lifted a hand, cupped her cheek, and stroked my fingers across her soft skin. She sighed into my touch, and it was all the confirmation I needed in the world. "I want to play the role of your man. I want to take you out. I want to spend more nights with you. I want us to be together and see where this goes, because I think we're only going to go to fantastic places." I gave her my best hopeful grin. "Because you and I—we go together so damn well."

She couldn't contain her smile either. She leaned into me, roping her hands around my neck and playing with the ends of my hair. "I'd say you've got the part."

I dropped my lips to hers and kissed her.

I'd felt possessive from the first night I touched her. But this time I could fully show her that, show her how much I wanted her for my own. This time, it wasn't only physical. It was so much more.

It was a promise of what I wanted us to become.

I kissed her hard, letting her know she was mine. When I broke the kiss, I ran a thumb over her bottom lip. "You're mine, Kate Williams."

"You bet I am," she said.

I laughed. "You and your bets."

"Speaking of bets, check your phone, Mr. Hamilton."

I dipped my hand into my back pocket for my phone and slid my thumb across the screen, reading her apology and, underlying that, her hope.

"I'll raise you," I said, in answer to her note. "In fact, I bet you'll be naked in my bed for the next several nights."

"I'll take that bet."

I tipped my head toward where Nina and Lily had gone to join the rest of their book club. "Want to go to your meeting?"

She shook her head, a naughty look in her pretty hazel eyes. "Not as much as I want to skip it and get naked with you."

"Best answer ever."

25

KATE

The message arrived on Friday afternoon.

Jake: Meet me at Edge. Here's the scenario. We're lovers, and we haven't seen each other in a month.

Kate: Does that mean we'll be climbing each other in seconds?

Jake: No, because we have to stay there until the check comes. How long can you last—that is the question.

* * *

He waited at the bar, drinking a scotch and looking insanely sexy with his dark hair, his five-o'clock shadow, and a button-down shirt that I wanted to rip off.

Or maybe he looked insanely sexy because of how he stared at me.

With hunger and with need. With dirty intent.

But with a little something else too.

Something tender.

Something that, if it was anything like what was happening to me, felt a little bit like falling.

That was what I was feeling for Jake Hamilton.

I walked over, licking my lips, savoring the sight of my man. As soon as I reached him, I went for it, pressing a kiss to his lips.

"It's been too long," I whispered.

"I couldn't agree more," he said, sliding a hand around my waist, grazing lower, squeezing my ass.

"Let's get out of here," I murmured, my skin heating in mere seconds from his touch.

His other hand traveled up my arm, along the back of my neck and into my hair. Tugging on my strands, he said, "But I have to take care of the check."

I arched into him. "Then you can take care of me."

"You bet I will," he growled, jerking me closer, sliding my body between his spread legs so I was pressed against the heavy weight of his erection through his slacks. I moaned as I felt his length, wanting him inside me.

He pulled me closer, knowing it was driving me wild to be this near to him. Lowering his head, he whispered in my ear, "I bet others are watching us."

"What do you think they're saying?" I asked, breathless, loving this new direction.

"They're saying, 'He's going to take her upstairs and

strip her to nothing in ten seconds flat.'"

I wriggled against him, aching. "They're saying, 'Doesn't it look like she's desperate for him?'"

"They're imagining I'm going to take you against the wall. They're betting as soon as the door closes, I'll hike up your skirt, tug down your panties, and slide my rock-hard cock inside you."

Lust slid down my spine as a shudder wracked me. "And I'll ask for deeper, harder, more."

"And I'll give it to you that way. Because I love nothing more than giving you all the pleasure in the world."

I ran my hands through his hair. "And I love it when you do."

Ten minutes later, the door to the room banged shut as Jake unzipped his pants, yanked up my skirt, and pushed inside me.

I cried out in absolute bliss.

This was the true decadent gift—this wicked, sinful indulgence as he took me to the ends of pleasure, sending me to ecstasy.

But what made it even better was what came next.

After, as we stumbled to the bed, wrapped up in each other, I ran my hands over his chest and said the hardest and easiest thing of all. "I'm falling in love with you, Jake Hamilton."

He pressed a kiss to my lips. "I'm falling in love with you too."

I was choosing to trust. Choosing to love. Choosing to take a chance.

That was the gift I gave myself.

26

TRISH

"That worked out quite well, I think," I told Christine, the pulsing music in the club covering our self-congratulations. Tonight, my dear friend and I celebrated a project that only affected a beloved few, but this city's boys' club mentality assumed the only plotting we ladies were up to was shoe-or-accessory related.

As if.

Christine raised her glass of champagne in a toast. "To brilliant ideas."

I clinked my glass against hers. "To brilliant partnerships."

"To brilliant women." She lifted her glass once more and took a deep drink.

I sipped the bubbly, grateful for friends like Christine Hamilton-Carey, and like Ivy Carmichael, who'd passed on a little tidbit about how happy Kate had seemed on Saturday night with her "friend."

A sexy man-friend who'd made her smile.

And I was glad of that.

I set my drink down with a knowing smile. "None of this subterfuge would have been necessary if they'd simply admitted that we always know what's best."

We checked out the scene at Edge from the lounge, where we were set up with a chilled bottle of bubbly and more breathing room than there was at the bar.

Christine shook her head. "So stubborn. It's a good thing we are benevolent fairy godmothers."

We toasted again and debriefed the last few weeks. For some time, I'd been watching Kate, my brilliant, irreplaceable Kate, peddling for all she was worth just to keep from losing ground on the mountain of trouble left by her last relationship. I could sense she was on the cusp of burning out, and I knew with a little help she could get over the hump. I'd made sure she was well paid for everything she did, but Sin City Escorts was an opportunity for me to give Kate the opportunity to gain traction with a hefty bonus. Was it on the generous side? That didn't matter nearly as much as the risk of losing her.

I wanted her to have everything she wanted in life because she was valuable to me. Not just for the business. She had a brilliant insight into people and what they wanted, what motivated them, but she was a kind, hardworking, honest woman who didn't deserve what her horrible ex had done to her.

But I didn't just want her to be able to pay off her debt. I wanted her to be happy.

And that was where Christine's brother had come in. I'd had a feeling about him.

Not *that* kind of feeling.

A feeling that had come from watching Kate when her group of friends made plans that included that man.

Christine crossed her legs. "You are a genius, Trish. There's nothing I want more than to see my little brother happy."

I arched a brow. "And what about you, darling? What are you going to do about *you* being happy?"

Christine simply shrugged. "Someday I'll find love again. When it's the right time, I'll feel it."

But love took more than a feeling, and it definitely took more than waiting around for "someday." If my friend didn't show some initiative, I would have to show some myself and find someone for her too. I'd already outlined a plan for just that possibility.

Sipping my champagne, I asked, "Have I ever introduced you to Daniel, my driver?"

"Your *driver?*" she asked, as if that was so incredible.

"Don't be a snob, darling."

Christine all but choked on her bubbly. "That's not what I meant."

I knew it wasn't, but I also knew she'd want to prove it and not reject the idea without consideration.

"He's quite handsome. He's friendly. His dog can ride with him on his motorcycle, which is too adorable for words."

"Apparently it isn't, since you have so much to say about it," she said with a bit of a smirk.

"He also owns the limo company."

"If he's all that, why don't you keep him for yourself, hmm?"

I smiled because she hadn't yet offered a real objection. "You know he's not my type," I said.

Christine patted me on the knee. "I know he's not."

She kicked her foot some more, watched the crowd, sipped her champagne, and I waited, doing much the same thing, but without making a silent pro and con list at the same time.

Finally, she drained her glass, and said, "All right, I'll do it."

"What was that?" I asked, cocking my ear her way. "I'm right, and you'll do as I say?"

She pretended to aim the very pointy toe of her pump at my shin, but of course her heart wasn't in it. "I said I'll meet your driver. You should be more gracious in victory."

"I know," I said solemnly. "Since I have so much practice at being right."

And I would be right about Daniel and Christine too. She, like the other women we had cultivated friendships or mutual interests with, did so much for so little credit. She deserved to be happy, and I had a feeling about Daniel.

Later, with a glow of satisfaction, I headed home. Annabelle was waiting for me to fix her supper, and there would be no snuggles if I came in too late.

Well, there would be snuggles eventually. Annabelle never held a grudge for long. That was the lovely thing about rescue spaniels. Nothing was so bad that a bowl of kibble and some tummy rubs couldn't fix it.

Humans could take a lesson from that.

27

CHRISTINE

I should never have said yes to the date.

Why did I say yes to this date?

Because of Trish. Because of Trish and her damn skill for persuasion.

I'd been on dates since Richard passed. Only two, but they stuck out like twin sore thumbs in my memory.

The first one, I'd started crying midway through the first drink. That was great.

The second one, well, there just hadn't been that *spark*.

Translation: the date was a dud, and I couldn't blame the guy.

Even though I couldn't remember his name.

But going 0 for two was enough to make me think I wasn't going to feel that spark again. I wasn't hung up on Richard. I'd mourned, I'd grieved, I'd gone to therapy. And with a lot of work, I'd been able to say good-bye. So it wasn't that I was hung up on him. Richard would've wanted me to date again. He'd even said so when he was first taken ill.

So perhaps the fault was mine.

The lack of spark was on me.

Maybe I didn't have it in me to go through it all again.

A heart that wasn't up for another beating.

Even if Trish convinced me to focus solely on the fun side of this date.

It'll be terrific! You'll get back out there! Trust me.

I just needed to get dressed. It was just a date, after all. Just fun. I needed to just get dressed and get it over with.

On the bathroom vanity, my phone buzzed. I grabbed it as I held the towel closer around my breasts.

And of course it was Trish. She could sense me giving up from a mile away. I swear the woman had friend radar. She was so damn sharp. She always knew when I needed a pick-me-up.

Trish: I'm waiting for an outfit pic. Can you see me twiddling my thumbs?

Christine: No. I don't have bionic vision.

A few seconds later a gif arrived of a woman twiddling thumbs. I knew an order when I saw one. But even so, I wasn't quite ready to follow it.

Christine: Confession: I can't do this.

Trish: Truth: Yes you can. Send the pic.

I glanced at the dress I'd laid out on my bed. It was tight and hugged me in all the places I liked. Plus, the pretty blue that perfectly matched my eyes.

The dress was ready for the date. But, was I?

Christine: What if it's terrible?

Trish: The outfit or the date?

Christine: Both.

A series of dots appeared as I waited for her response. Then, a message appeared that made me laugh in a way only Trish could. She was taking my worries step by step. Just like her.

Trish: Let's start with the outfit. We can tackle world issues next.

Time to say fuck it to nerves.

This was it. No more second-guessing.

Just *do*.

I slid on the dress and headed for the inner sanctum – my shoe shelves.

After digging through piles of tennis shoes and reasonable heels for work, I fished out a pair of stilettos. Then I paused when I spotted a pair of basic black pumps. Should I go with something more sensible?

Nope, this wasn't a night for business meetings.

This was a night for possibility.

Stilettos for the win.

Red. High. Daring.

After all, maybe the shoes would deactivate the nerves.

It could happen. Shoes had been known to possess superpowers.

I snapped a selfie in the mirror and sent it off to Trish. Almost immediately, several enthusiastic fire emojis landed on my screen.

Trish: Daniel's dead. He won't be able to handle how hot you are!

Christine: Have I told you that I'm keeping you forever as a friend?

Trish: I know you are.

Turning, I caught a glimpse of myself in the mirror. I had to admit, the dress did look great on me. Even before I'd had Carson, I'd always had a good ass. Lucky that way, I suppose. Tonight, my booty was emphasized in a way that even upstaged my magical yoga leggings.

I imagined Daniel seeing me in this dress. Where would his eyes go first? Would he be one of those guys who didn't even bother to look at your face? Who surveyed your assets?

And more to the point, where would my eyes travel on him?

I'd seen Daniel before on the occasional limo ride with Trish, and I'd be lying if I said I hadn't noticed the sharpness of his jawline and the way his green eyes danced in the rearview mirror when he looked back at me.

Was that why I'd given in to Trish? No, it was more.

Trish had a special talent for people. An eye for connection.

I hoped, against all odds, she might be right about Daniel and me.

I looked in the mirror again. I swiped on a red lipstick I hadn't put on in ages. It had never felt right for the boardroom. Too much, they would have said. Even for my line of work.

But tonight?

It seemed perfect for possibility.

* * *

Jake and Carson were already settled on the couch with a pair of controllers. They didn't hear me come into the living room, so I stood at the edge and watched as Carson waved at the screen.

"Just hit the square and R1!" Carson said, bouncing up and down. "That'll make him do a low cross. See? Watch me."

In a flash, Carson made his soccer player on the screen kick the ball across and into the goal. Next to him, Jake stared open-mouthed. In real life, I bet Jake could've mastered that low cross kick.

But here?

Carson was king.

And he was loving it.

"You're not clicking fast enough," Carson explained.

"Maybe you're right and thirty really *is* too old," Jake said, laughing and ruffling Carson's hair with his free hand.

Carson grinned. "It's okay. I can teach you. Remember? I'm the master."

Behind them, I cleared my throat so that they both turned around.

"Well look at you," Jake said. "You look great, sis."

I bit my lip. "It's not too much?"

"No way!" Carson said, jumping off the couch. "Mom, you look pretty. Well, for a mom."

I laughed, and that was helpful, because I refused to cry in front of him, even though his comment, caveat and all, already had me tearing up. I held out my arms so he could run over and hug me.

"Thank you," I said as we let go.

Carson gave me one last grin before he rushed back to the couch and grabbed the controller again. My brother came over, glancing at him before looking at me.

"So," he said, sounding pleased. "You're finally taking that 'me time' you so generously encouraged me to take."

I laughed. "Your 'me time' didn't really last. Pretty sure it's turned into you-and-Kate time."

Jake grinned. "Can't say I regret that in the least. And who's to say that won't happen with you and Daniel?"

I couldn't help it. I smiled. Then, Carson let out a whoop from the couch, and my heart flipped just a little.

"Are you sure he's okay with this?" I asked, in a whisper, nerves kicking back up.

Jake's expression softened. "Christine," he said, squeezing my arm. "You saw him just now. He wants you to be happy."

I took in a deep breath. He was right. And I hated that he was. Who gave my little brother permission to be the smart one?

"Besides," Jake said, nudging me in the shoulder. "If I get to—what was it you said?—*sparkle*, then so should you."

I pinched his cheek. "And you are very sparkly."

In my pocket, my phone buzzed. Daniel. I'd asked him to text me when he was outside. I wasn't ready for him to knock and meet Jake and Carson.

Not yet, anyway.

For now, I was doing this on my terms, just like everything else in my life.

"He's here," I said to Jake. "Now go back and be a good babysitter. And don't let him play video games all night."

My brother winked before returning to Carson and the low cross.

Leaving me to slip out the door.

Leaving me to my new chance in the city of opportunity.

* * *

For the briefest moment before I opened the door, I panicked and wondered if Daniel would have come on his motorcycle. I had no idea how I was supposed to ride a motorcycle in a tight dress.

But when I glanced down the driveway, I saw something better. A limo, long and sleek. He stood in front of it, a tailored suit jacket skimming his thick arms and broad shoulders. His dark hair was just the right amount of messy.

Even without the motorcycle, he'd arrived looking both put together and a little wild.

The thought made me imagine sitting behind him, my arms wrapped around him.

His muscles moving under my hands as I held on.

The wind zipping past us as we roared down the Vegas Strip.

I shook off the thought.

No motorcycle for tonight. And in my stilettos, that was probably for the best.

"I trust you're Christine?" Daniel asked as I approached, holding out his hand. A polite gentleman. I guessed he would have to be to be good enough to work for Trish.

"You trust correctly."

"Then this is already the best blind date I've ever been on," he said, and I couldn't help but smile.

He brought my hand to his lips, brushing a kiss against my knuckles as he met my gaze with his. Something dangerous and exciting glinted in his eyes.

Well. Maybe not such a gentleman after all.

And judging from the way my shoulders tingled, maybe that wasn't such a bad idea.

"Hello," I said and glanced back at the limo. "You're not driving, are you?"

He let out a deep, throaty laugh that made me shiver down to my toes. I had to get it together. Daniel was just a man. Just a first date.

So why did his simple laugh turn me on? Or maybe he did already.

"One of the perks of owning a limo company is getting to take them out occasionally," he said with a warm smile. "We'll be in the back. I have some champagne if you'd like. Or water. Soda. Or tea. I like to come prepared."

I kind of loved that. His presentation of options.

"Champagne sounds fantastic."

He smiled, and I smiled back, feeling as giddy and bubbly as what we were about to drink.

He opened the door for me, and I slipped inside. It smelled like clean leather and his cologne—musky and rich—and I shivered a little as he slid in next to me.

He reached for the bottle of champagne and poured me a glass. The whole time, I watched how sure and steady his movements were.

How he gripped the bottle with purpose.

It made it easy to imagine his hands on me.

Hmm. Maybe I was more ready for this date than I thought. Or maybe my body was saying I was ready for other things too.

That didn't sound like such a bad idea.

"So, Christine," he said, watching me with intense and knowing eyes. "Are you ready for tonight?"

I breathed. Was I?

"Yes," I said, meeting his gaze "I absolutely am."

He smiled, passing me the glass and clinking it against his.

"To new beginnings," he toasted, and I repeated it before tipping it back.

* * *

On the way over, we traded questions back and forth, chatting about work and the city.

"Tell me about the life of a Las Vegas limo driver," I said, finding talking with him surprisingly comfortable. He had a way about him of putting me at ease.

"This might sound odd, but the city feels like a friend."

"How so?"

"It listens to me," he said, and when I raised an eyebrow, he laughed.

"No, really," he insisted. "Sometimes, if there's traffic, I'll ask it if it could just let me through a little faster. And it does."

"That can't be true," I said, but I was grinning.

"Maybe I'm just magic," he said with a roguish wink.

"Maybe you are. Lucky man." I took a beat. "So you're the owner who likes driving. I suppose at the risk of sounding obvious, does it ever get exhausting?"

He shrugged. "I like the peace. Helping people get to their destinations. And I'm lucky because I have good clients."

"Like Trish?" I asked.

"Trish is great. She's always got a plan. Or a scheme."

I smiled a little shyly. "Like with setting us up?"

Daniel rubbed his chin, quiet at first. But his eyes sort of twinkled. Something was clearly on his mind.

"Truth be told, that was only partly Trish's scheme," he said, his voice confident, a little lower than before. "The other part was me."

At first, I thought he was joking. But when I looked again, he was serious.

"It was? Your idea?"

He tapped his chest, owning it. "My idea. What can I say? There was one time when I drove you and Trish, and I couldn't stop watching you. Usually, I'm able to tune out whatever's happening behind me. But with you, I had to watch. I was compelled."

I blushed at his words. "You're kidding."

He shook his head. "You're lovely, Christine."

And that tingle I felt earlier turned into a full-blown swoon.

"Thank you. I don't know what to say, except thank you."

"Thank you for saying yes. I was hooked on your laugh the very first time I heard it. You laughed like the world was there for the taking. And the way you could hold your own. You know what you want, and I'll be honest with you, Christine."

"Yes?" I asked, and I felt as if I were on the edge of my seat.

He stared at me, the scent of champagne lingering between us. It was going to my head in all the good ways.

He leveled me with a sexy stare. "I wanted you to want *me*."

The limo slowed and then came to a halt, and Daniel smiled as he leaned back again.

His confidence shocked me.

Thrilled me, honestly.

I'd never had a man be so bold on a first date.

But Daniel said those words as if he were telling me about the weather.

But I couldn't let him off that easily. What if this was a line? I was no college girl out for her first date with a real man. I was a grown woman, owner of a successful company. I'd been around the block a few times.

If he thought it would be that easy, he was wrong.

"I'm glad to hear that," I said, a little playful, as the driver opened my door. "But I guess you'll have to give me a reason to want you, then."

And just then, something hit me. Something wonderful. I was getting my groove back. I was flirting. I was having fun.

Daniel laughed. "I fully intend to."

Before I knew it, he'd come around to take my hand as I stepped out onto the sidewalk. I let his hand linger on mine as he walked me to the front doors of the Delano Las Vegas Hotel. The building shimmered and the palm trees around us swayed gently in the breeze.

But the shiver I felt wasn't just from the night air.

It was from Daniel, still holding on to my hand as we walked into the hotel.

Right away, I could tell that the Delano was all about decadence in a way that only Vegas could do. We took the elevator all the way to the top to Rivea, a restaurant I'd heard about but had never had a special enough occasion to go to.

Now, I did.

As soon as we entered, my eyes drank in the beauty. The chandelier in the center looked like water frozen mid-air, though Daniel said it was actually handblown glass.

"Just wait until we get outside," he told me, touching my lower back as he guided us inside. "It's the best view in Vegas."

"We'll see about that," I teased. "You're setting some high standards tonight."

The devilish grin made another appearance. "And I intend to meet all of them."

And a shiver stole up my spine again.

What was it about this man that undid me so easily?

I would focus on dinner, I decided. Just because this was my first date back on the scene didn't mean I needed to be so easily won over.

* * *

Lucky for me, dinner was delectable, and I was sure you couldn't go wrong with burrata with heritage tomatoes, or mouth-watering lobster risotto. As I ate, he watched me like I was a painting he wanted to memorize. I wasn't used to that, but I found I loved being on display for him. I craned my neck and tossed my hair over my shoulder.

Hell, I even fluttered my eyelashes at him.

Maybe I was being silly.

Mostly, I felt free.

He made me feel like I should as he tossed questions at me. He wanted to know about Carson, about my business, where and how Trish and I had met.

He genuinely wanted to know me. "Tell me more about yourself," I asked him midway through our meal. "I feel like I've done all the talking."

Mostly, because Daniel had nothing but earnest, kind questions. "I guess I should start with the most important part of my life."

He pulled his phone out of his pocket and picked out a picture from his camera roll. A candid shot of the happiest looking dog I'd ever seen in my life. It was some kind of mix, maybe part French bulldog and part corgi?

"That's Harmony," Daniel explained. "She's a rescue.

All my dogs have been rescued. It's sort of my side job. And sometimes, the tougher cases end up staying with me. Like Harmony."

He pointed in the picture so that I saw that Harmony only had one eye.

My heart thumped. "Aww. You gave her a home?"

"I couldn't help it when I heard about her," Daniel explained. "Most of the dogs I rescue, I find homes for. But with Harmony, I saw her in her little cage and I just knew. I had to save her. I had to make sure she'd never feel alone like that again."

What can I say? My heart didn't just thump. It melted.

Completely.

Right there and then.

"She's adorable," I admitted.

He grinned. "She's my girl. She's the one Trish told you about, my little motorcycle rider. Found her in a warehouse six years ago, and she's been by my side ever since."

"I'd love to meet her," I said, and I meant it.

"I think she'd like you," Daniel said. "Though it might be hard to get her to share the motorcycle."

"Oh?" I arched a brow. "And what if I want a ride alone with you?"

I hadn't meant it to sound like *that*, but Daniel's eyes immediately darkened and his grin widened.

"That could always be arranged."

I rolled my eyes, trying to deflect from my unexpected flirtiness. "You know what I mean."

Before he could respond, the waiter arrived with a

dessert menu. I scanned it, my eyes catching on the limoncello baba and chocolate soufflé. I hesitated.

"Something wrong?" Daniel asked.

"No," I said, but then I looked at his eyes and decided I could be honest. "It's just that I've never thought that these fancy restaurants can ever get dessert quite right."

He lifted an eyebrow. "Really?"

"Maybe it's just how I was raised. But for me, nothing beats soft serve ice cream. Plain old regular soft serve."

Daniel's brow furrowed like he was deep in thought. "A twist? Vanilla? Chocolate?"

I laughed. "Thinking of running out and getting some?"

He shook his head. "No. I'm planning our next date."

This man and his confidence were going to be the end of me. We were barely done with our first meal together and he was already planning another one.

He definitely wasn't serving up lines.

I bit my lip, deciding to keep having fun. "How do you know there's a next date?"

Daniel made a move as if I'd gravely offended him.

"I thought you wanted to meet Harmony?"

Now, it was my turn for faux-outrage. "Using your dog as leverage?"

He grinned wickedly. "Whatever it takes."

Everything just felt so easy around him.

I couldn't stop looking at his mouth, at the even row of teeth and those full lips.

I could just imagine how they'd feel on my mouth.

My neck.

Me.

"Time for the view," Daniel said, reaching for my hand. "If you're sure you're prepared?"

I nodded, letting him lead me outside. It was dark, but the lights of Vegas never slept. They dotted the horizon, and outside, we could see all of the hotels in the city.

He was right. It *was* the best view in Vegas.

As I looked, Daniel settled in next to me. His arm extended around me, and I gave in and leaned against him and breathed in his scent.

"It's beautiful," I whispered.

"So are you," he whispered back, his lips brushing against my ear.

I turned to look at him. He watched me from those beautiful eyes, glittering in the lights of Vegas.

"I have another confession," I said.

"More dessert preferences?" Daniel asked.

I shook my head. "I noticed you too. Not exactly like you noticed me. But I did. That's why I agreed when Trish suggested you."

He watched me. "Now that you're on a date with me, what do you think? Do I live up to your expectations?"

I caught my breath.

This is it, I thought.

The moment I cross from possibility into reality.

"I think we should've done this sooner," I said. "*Much* sooner."

I lifted my chin, parted my lips and waited.

But not for long.

We both knew what was happening next.

He cupped my cheek, and brushed his lips to mine.

His were so soft, so sweet that I sighed.

A soft, little sigh.

And as the sound ghosted across my lips, I felt myself giving in more.

To the kiss. To the feel of his mouth exploring mine. To his hand on my face.

And most of all, to the lovely thrill of a wonderful first date that I was clearly ready for.

In fact, I was ready for the next one as soon as possible.

* * *

Still in a daze by the time I returned home, I slipped quietly in through the front door and into the living room. Jake was asleep on the couch, a book open on his lap and Carson passed out on his shoulder.

My little brother, babysitter extraordinaire.

I should wake them up and get Carson into his bed, but I figured that, while they slept, I might as well get into the shower.

I still needed to stop buzzing after my date, after all.

I tiptoed to my bedroom and ran the hot water, unzipping my dress as I remembered how Daniel's hands had felt along the exposed skin.

How his kiss had felt.

How my mouth felt deliciously bruised in a way it hadn't felt in years.

As I started to pull the dress off my shoulders, my phone buzzed. I glanced at it and laughed.

Of course it was Trish.

Trish: Okay, I can't take it anymore. How was it?

I thought about Daniel's hands in the dark, how his palm had grazed my thigh in the limo, daring me not to cry out and alert the driver.

How, even after that, he'd been the perfect gentleman who walked me to my door.

How he was somehow wicked and wild, sensitive and caring.

Everything I could've hoped for and more.

Christine: I can't lie to you. You were right.

I could practically hear Trish whooping in the distance, and when she sent back several winking emojis, I knew she'd be asking for more details soon. Before she could, another text popped up.

One that made my heart stop and start at the same time.

Daniel: I can't stop thinking about you.

I bit my lip and glanced in the mirror. The lace of my bra was visible, peeking out of the piece of the dress I'd started to pull down. My lipstick was smeared slightly from our kisses, and my hair was tangled around my shoulders.

I could just take off the dress, step into the shower, and wash away the night.

But Daniel couldn't stop thinking about me.

And I didn't want him to stop.

I took a picture of myself in the mirror and then fired it off to Daniel before I could second-guess myself.

Tonight had been everything.

And I intended to enjoy every last second that I could.

28

KATE

A year later

"C'mon! Beat that high score!"

I cheered on my boyfriend and his nephew as they competed in a pinball competition.

I had a feeling they were going to win. The two of them had been on a tear as pinball teammates in the last year, and I was so damn proud of them both.

A few seconds later, the pinball machine lit up, and the Hamiltonians, as they called themselves, hit a new high score.

I screamed my heart out, along with my vocal cords. But that was par for the course around Jake. My vocal cords always seemed to get a workout with my man.

When the competition ended, I jumped into his arms, giving him a big, wet kiss. When I let go, I high-fived Carson, then I fist-bumped Christine.

"Our boys rock," I said.

"That they do," she seconded. Then she turned to her boyfriend. In the last year, she'd started dating again, and had found happiness with Daniel.

Turned out Trish had played a part in that relationship too.

My boss had quite the cupid in her, I'd learned.

But that wasn't surprising.

Trish was the queen of this city, and she was a deal-maker. There was nothing she loved better than to seal the bargain, whether in business or love.

* * *

We said good night to the three of them after the tournament, and Jake and I went to one of our favorite spots —the scene of our first "scene."

The Rapture.

We'd played many parts here in the last year, acted out many scenarios—pilot and flight attendant, boss and assistant, teacher and student.

And we'd invented scenarios for many others.

It was the place where we'd fallen into bed and fallen in love. For us, those two things were intertwined.

As they should be.

As we wound down the hall of The Extravagant toward the music pulsing from inside the club, Jake squeezed my hand. "What role do you want to play tonight?"

I tapped my chin, contemplating our options. "How about—"

I blinked, because Jake had disappeared from my

peripheral vision. But he hadn't actually vanished. At the speed of light, Jake had bent down on one knee, and I found him holding a small velvet box. His gaze locked with mine, his dark-brown eyes so vulnerable.

"There's one more important role I'd like to play with you. Kate Williams, you are brilliant and beautiful, captivating and kind, sexy and sinful, the most wonderful friend, and the most incredible lover. The only other role I want you to play is my wife. Will you marry me?"

I dropped to my knees too, threw my arms around him, and said yes.

"I'll take you up on that offer," I said. "And I'll bet we'll make it last for all time."

"I'll take that wager." He slid a gorgeous diamond on my finger as tears of happiness streamed down my cheeks, and the future seemed like the surest bet of all.

Later, our friends joined us at the club to celebrate. Adam bought a bottle of champagne and toasted to us, claiming he was responsible for the union.

I didn't see a need to correct him.

Besides, Jake had told me what Adam had said, and he had played a part after all.

So many people had their own roles in getting us together, and I felt so lucky that they did. And how lucky was it that I'd decided to explore my fantasies that weekend?

Now we'd have a lifetime of doing just that.

As I drew Jake in for another kiss, I caught a glimpse of a familiar face on the dance floor.

It belonged to a man who had played a part during a meaningful time in my life when he'd shared his thoughts on companionship, friendship, and kindness.

The top escort for one of my biggest clients was dancing with the maid of honor from that fateful girls' night out.

And I was dying to know what their story was.

29

ANTONY

I straightened my tie and adjusted my collar, which was just showing above the neck of the black graduation gown.

I shifted my weight, the shoes I'd polished last night gleaming in the light. Old-fashioned, maybe, but something I'd never stopped doing for myself. My father had taught me, and he'd learned in the army. A spit shine was a lost art, even if it was hardly rocket science.

I'd heard some variation of the "it's not rocket science" joke 457 times since starting school.

"Worth it," I told my reflection in the mirror of the cloak room at the university. I looked like an aerospace engineer, I decided, adjusting the stole-type thing so the point was straight on my chest and the hood draped down my back. "Nerdy and a little like a professor at Hogwarts," I declared.

I joined the other master's degree candidates in the hall outside the auditorium. My classmates had clumped up to exchange good wishes before we lined up in alphabetical order. There weren't a large number of us, and some had been in class together since their undergraduate days. I considered myself lucky to have made the friends I did, especially since I'd always worked weekends.

I imagined I'd work plenty of weekends as a junior engineer too. I bet it would be a lot quieter though. Probably lonelier too. I might miss that part of my job— the escort part of escorting.

It was a strange world, and I was immensely grateful for the luck I'd had and all the opportunities that had led me to where I was. Not the least of which was a job that allowed me to pay for school and arrange my schedule around classes.

I had just one more job this weekend, and then I'd be trading Sin City Escorts for a whole new kind of city living – the regular kind.

The familiar strains of "Pomp and Circumstance" began, and the line of graduates processed into the auditorium. Later, I would consider the near and far future. Now it was time to cross the stage, shake the dean's hand, and get my diploma.

This was what I'd dreamed of many years ago.

And many times over the last several months.

This moment was here at last.

* * *

The Saturday morning of my last job for Sin City Escorts, I picked up my shirts from the laundry and chose a tie for my final assignment. I was feeling nostalgic. I never liked goodbyes. Ironic, with a ships-that-pass-in-the-night kind of business like this, but that was how it went.

I was ready to move on though. Sure, some aspects of the job I enjoyed, and I didn't have much to complain about. But the reality was, I'd stopped differentiating between clients, and when I was with someone—however I was with her—I tried to be present. That was hard when the jobs ran together.

It was through no fault of the women. But a job was a job after all.

The one woman who stood out, though, was Sidney from Phoenix. A year ago, she'd been visiting Vegas and she'd hired me, or maybe her friend had. We'd spent the evening just talking. That was all. We'd started at a bar in The Luxe, then wound up at a noodle joint, eating and laughing and talking. That was where she'd told me her hopes and dreams, her aspirations . . . her wish to become an environmental scientist, her wish to adopt a rescue dog, her wish to be loved.

I'd had a feeling it had been a while since anyone had truly listened to her. The way she'd opened up had forged an intimacy between us, and that was likely why I remembered her.

When she'd smiled, her green eyes had twinkled, and I could still remember that look in them.

So when I opened up the details of tonight's assignment in my inbox, I grinned.

My eyes were probably twinkling too.

Because I could sure as hell recognize a cosmic

confluence, even if I was an engineer and not an astronomer.

Tonight's client was Sidney from Phoenix.

The one who hadn't fallen from my mind.

Hell no. She hadn't fallen out of my head one bit.

* * *

Wow.

Just wow.

As I walked into the bar at The Venetian, I had one thought.

Sidney was more lovely than I'd remembered.

Or possibly more lovely, period. When we'd first met, she'd seemed a bit brittle. Not her personality, but her emotions, almost as if they were pottery fired in an oven too long and a hard knock might shatter her.

But as I joined her, dropping a kiss on her soft cheek, the woman with me now seemed resilient, with rosy color in her face and a newfound liveliness in those eyes—as if the sparkle in them was no longer fleeting. It was regular.

"How have you been?" she asked, and she sounded like a good friend, someone I hadn't seen in a while.

"Terrific. And you?"

"I'm well." The smile she flashed was bright and genuine.

We made small talk while we waited for the server to bring our drinks, and it felt more like a date than work.

Was it because this was my last assignment? Because I'd checked out of this job already?

Or was it because of her?

The only one I hadn't ejected from my mind.

The one who'd stood out.

And I had my answer.

It was her.

Though this was my last job, I felt anything but disengaged.

After the waiter brought our drinks, Sidney ran her finger along the rim of the glass. "I suppose you're wondering why I asked for you tonight. Besides the obvious."

Her blush hinted at what she meant, but I didn't feel like rushing to get there. I'd be disappointed if we did. I wanted to take my time with her.

"I never assume anything is obvious," I said, and then surprised myself by asking, "Why don't you start by telling me how you've been doing the past year? I want to hear more about you."

Her lips curved slowly into another smile. "Well, I graduated, for one thing. Master's in environmental science."

"Congratulations, then. You were looking forward to working in that field, I recall." I raised my glass, toasting her.

"I was. I am. I'm touched you remembered."

I leaned a little closer. "I just graduated too," I said, then I blinked.

What the hell was that? I just shared a detail of my private life, and I never did that.

"Ah! What a coincidence!"

Sidney didn't notice anything amiss. She wouldn't, because she hadn't worked as an escort and kept her private details private, at the peril of . . . well, unlikely but terrible things.

"What were you studying?" she asked.

I supposed it didn't matter now. No need to keep my real life under lock and key. "Aerospace engineering."

Her eyes widened with obvious delight. "So you're a . . ."

"Go ahead and say it." I gestured in invitation. "Get it out of your system."

Her grin was full of mischief. "I'll save it for when you're not expecting it."

"I'm always expecting that joke." I sipped my drink. "But go on. Catch me up on life in Phoenix."

"For one thing, I'm not in Phoenix anymore." She slid her glass around on the table, leaving a trail of condensation. "I've moved here."

Surprise after surprise tonight. That just didn't happen often. Not while still sitting in the bar, at least. "Have you really?" I asked, trying hard to rein in a grin.

Or perhaps not trying hard to at all.

Because it seemed like a damn fine coincidence too.

"I have indeed." She tucked her chin almost shyly and looked at me through her lashes. It could have been annoyingly coy, but on Sidney it was sweet and genuine, and just like her. "Antony . . . is it too early to ask to go up to my room?"

My muscles tensed briefly. The reminder of why I was here was unwelcome. Yes, the thought of going up to her room was hugely appealing, but not for the reasons she likely thought.

I didn't want to go up as an escort.

I wanted to go up as . . . her date.

And that wasn't anything I'd ever experienced before.

But I was still on the clock, and I'd been taught to respect not only my employer but also the client. Still, was she ready? Truly ready? She hadn't been before. I considered it part of my job to make sure the client was comfortable at all times, and sometimes that meant I needed to apply the brakes for a smoother ride.

"If you want to go up, it's not too early. But what if we were to finish our drinks and then decide?"

She nodded, then whispered, "Of course." She looked down, biting her lip, and I worried that she took that as a rejection.

So I reached across the table and laid my hand on her arm, a spark of pleasure rushing through my body at the touch. Her skin was hot, as if she'd blushed all the way to her fingertips.

"Sidney, that wasn't a no," I explained. "That was a 'let's pretend you're not paying for my time.' I don't want to rush"—I didn't want to be on the clock at all, I was realizing—"and maybe you want to sort some things out yourself."

Her glance came at me sideways this time. Always dancing, her green eyes. Even when she seemed a little peeved. "I know you didn't just say that I don't know my own mind," she said, her tone strong.

"I wouldn't dare." Tracing my thumb over the skin of

her arm, I made sure I had her attention. "It's just that last year, you weren't ready. That wasn't your speed."

"Last year," she said sharply, "I'd just found out my asshole boyfriend had been cheating on me with half of Phoenix." Some of the sting in those words seemed to be aimed at me, perhaps for presuming to know her mind. "So, I was having a few trust and intimacy issues," she added.

"Understandable." My tone was as unprovoking as I could make it. "And I didn't mean to suggest that you don't know what you want. That's not what I meant at all. What I meant was I wanted to make sure going upstairs was exactly what you wanted. Here," I said, dusting a fingertip over her temple. "And here." I touched her chest ever so lightly. "And everywhere." I took the liberty to run my hand along her waist, feeling her shudder into my touch.

When I reached her waist, she took my hand, clasping it. "Thank you for saying that. And let me speak my mind fully too. Because the thing is," she said, stopping to take a breath, "I've been thinking about that night for a year, wondering if I'd made a mistake. You listened to me ramble, and you were kind and funny, and I really enjoyed talking to you. Most of all, you seemed to see me. No matter who else you'd been with, I felt important to you then. That's a gift, making people feel cared for when you've just met."

That might have been the most a woman has said about me—me, not my looks or my skill or my stamina —in all the time I'd been doing this.

"It seems like you saw me that night too," I said, lacing our fingers more tightly together.

"We're impressive," she said with a gleam in her eye, "seeing that much when we didn't even get naked."

"Amazing what you can see when you're truly looking at everything," I said, our gazes locked as the air between us seemed charged, electric.

"Yes, everything," she repeated, then licked her lips.

And it seemed we were both ready.

It seemed she was ready to take a chance she wasn't ready to take a year ago.

And I wanted to take a different type of chance.

A chance at someone seeing beyond what they'd paid for.

We finished our drinks and made our unhurried way to the elevators, talking about the city, our new jobs, the rescue dog she wanted to adopt.

As we neared her door and she took out her key card, my heart hammered. I couldn't go in there as an escort. I had to tell her. Had to let her know this was different.

I drew her to a stop, turning her to face me and brushing her cheek with my fingers. "Sidney from Phoenix, the woman I couldn't get out of my mind, I don't want this to be a job."

She covered my fingers with hers, pressing them to her soft skin, her eyes locked with mine. "Then don't think of it as your job, and I won't think of it that way either."

I slid my other hand into her hair, cradling her head

and bringing her close. "It seems so simple when you put it that way."

"Well," she whispered when our lips were a breath apart, "it's not rocket science."

That settled it. I had to punish her mouth with a kiss.

* * *

I woke up with the feeling someone was staring at me.

Sidney, once from Phoenix, now from here.

She lay on her stomach, her chin on her hands, watching me with sleepy eyes. "I can't quite believe you did that."

I stretched my arms over my head. "You're going to have to narrow down what 'that' is. There are a lot of variables."

"You stayed the night."

"Is that okay?" It had felt so damn good to close my eyes with her snuggled against me, dynamite couldn't have blasted me out of this bed.

"Definitely."

I tucked some of her tumbled hair behind her ear. "I had to stay until you woke because I needed to ask if I can see you again."

Her mouth dropped open, and emotions flickered on her face too fast to read. "I would love to see you again." Her expression settled between wary and hopeful. "I might go broke, but it would be worth it."

"Lucky for you, as of this morning, I'm a cheap date." She frowned in confusion, and I suddenly felt tentative as I explained, "As of this morning, I am one-hundred-percent engineer and zero percent escort. Last night was my last job."

She considered that long enough for me to worry, tapping her chin. "How cheap?"

"What?" I frowned. Had I misread the whole night?

But a grin seemed to tug at her lips. "Because we're both new graduates, Antony. And I just made an extravagant purchase from my savings account. I need to watch my wallet now."

No way was I taking money for last night. I'd make sure Sin City didn't charge her. I dropped a kiss on her nose. "You're not paying for last night. I'll cover you. And tonight, I'd like to take you out." I pulled back to look at her, to watch her face transform from playful to vulnerable.

"You meant all that? About this not being a job?"

"Couldn't you tell? From the way we were together?"

She swallowed, then answered, "I know you said it. And I could tell what I wanted. But I didn't want to presume anything."

I ran a hand down her bare skin, savoring the feel of her soft, sexy body. "Then let me make it abundantly clear. I want you. I want to date you. I want to see you. I want to be the aerospace engineer to your environmental scientist." I took a beat, nerves thrumming through me. "That is, if you think you could let a former escort into your heart?"

Her smile widened like the sky. "You're already there."

"Good. That's where I'd like to stay."

The Extravagant, joining the justice of the peace, I barely saw them.

As the music played, I only had eyes for my bride.

The woman who'd be playing the role of my wife, my lover, and my best friend forever.

As she walked down the aisle, looking radiant in white, I knew I was the luckiest man in the world.

She was the greatest gift.

And the most decadent one.

THE END

Intrigued by Ivy Carmichael? She has a story of her own as she falls for her bodyguard. And her sister Sage will also have a romance. Stay tuned for **THE EXTRAVA-GANT GIFT and THE EXQUISITE GIFT**.

Sign up for my VIP After Dark mailing list here and don't miss a release!

Up next! You don't want to miss the release of MY SINFUL NIGHTS, the sizzling new reimagining of SWEET SINFUL NIGHTS!
Remember Edge? The club the friends go to in The Decadent Gift? It's owned by Brent Nichols and his romance has been completely rewritten with a brand new approach to the romance, the conflict and the

emotions and a story now told in first person. This scorching romantic suspense is available everywhere!

An excerpt follows...

Brent

Perfection.

That was how I'd always described kissing her. That was what I said to her after our lips met. Now, she slid off the stool, into my space.

Exactly where I wanted her.

Neither one of us said a word. Her green eyes were dark and intense. Her lips were so close. The inches between us were swallowed whole by the connection that crackled hot. She seemed to sway closer, and I moved in, seizing the moment.

I lifted my hand to her hair, pulled back in a messy bun, different from the shade she'd had when I knew her, but beautiful just the same. A strand had fallen loose, chestnut brown and curled. I touched it, ran my finger across the single lock. Time melted away as I leaned into the familiar crook of her neck. The craving for her ran so damn deep it lived inside my bones.

I inhaled her, that honey scent, a new smell that imprinted on me in an instant.

"Shan," I whispered, rough and gravelly, filled with so much want for her, which had built over the years, grown higher, spread farther, formed roots. Inhabited me. I was desperate to have her in my arms again, to smother her in kisses that erased all the years.

"Brent," she whispered, my name sounding like sugar on her tongue.

I buried my face in her neck, layering kisses on her soft skin. "Where have you been?" I asked, though it was entirely rhetorical. She hadn't been with me. I hadn't been with her. That was the answer.

"Where were you?" she countered softly.

I lifted my face and looked her in the eyes as I brushed the back of my fingers along her cheek. "Thinking of you," I said. I cupped her cheeks in my hands. "You're so fucking beautiful," I rasped out, and then I crushed my mouth to hers. I consumed her lips. I kissed her hard and greedily, and the world around me faded into a speck of nothingness because there was room for nothing else in my world but her. Nothing but the utter perfection of Shannon Paige-Prince wrapped around me where she belonged.

No time had passed.

No years had gone by.

No regrets had dug deep inside me.

We kissed like it was the first time, and the last time, and like it was for all time. We kissed like two people who wanted to climb into each other's skin, to smash into the other person. It was crashing back into orbit. It was gravity reinstated. In the press of her lips, in the slide of her tongue, in the gasps she made, we hurtled back in time. All mistakes were erased in that moment. There were no doubts. No questions. She had to feel everything I felt. She had to want a second chance too. I dropped a hand to her lower back, yanking her close, but not close enough. Kissing was not enough. Lips would only get us so far. I had to feel her, touch her, taste her.

She pressed into me, a full-body collision, grinding against me. I groaned as I reclaimed her mouth, my entire being consumed with a desire so powerful I didn't know how I'd make it through the rest of the day.

As she rubbed her body against me, I imagined the heat between her legs. It fried my brain and short-circuited my skull. The desire to touch her enveloped me. I wanted to watch her undress, to stare at that to-die-for body that I'd missed so terribly, to roam my eyes over her curves.

To touch her everywhere.

To have her, take her.

Hell, the way she fused her body to mine told me all I needed to know. She wanted the same things.

I kissed a line along her jaw to her ear as she breathed hard. "What do you say we have a do-over of last night?"

Preorder this scorching romance at an extreme discount everywhere!

ALSO BY LAUREN BLAKELY

FULL PACKAGE, the #1 New York Times Bestselling romantic comedy!

BIG ROCK, the hit New York Times Bestselling standalone romantic comedy!

THE SEXY ONE, a New York Times Bestselling standalone romance!

THE KNOCKED UP PLAN, a multi-week USA Today and Amazon Charts Bestselling standalone romance!

MOST VALUABLE PLAYBOY, a sexy multi-week USA Today Bestselling sports romance! And its companion sports romance, MOST LIKELY TO SCORE!

WANDERLUST, a USA Today Bestselling contemporary romance!

COME AS YOU ARE, a Wall Street Journal and multi-week USA Today Bestselling contemporary romance!

PART-TIME LOVER, a multi-week USA Today Bestselling contemporary romance!

UNBREAK MY HEART, an emotional second chance USA Today Bestselling contemporary romance!

BEST LAID PLANS, a sexy friends-to-lovers USA Today

Bestselling romance!

The Heartbreakers! The USA Today and WSJ Bestselling rock star series of standalone!

CONTACT

I love hearing from readers! You can find me on Twitter at LaurenBlakely3, Instagram at LaurenBlakelyBooks, Facebook at LaurenBlakelyBooks, or online at Lauren-Blakely.com. You can also email me at laurenblakely-books@gmail.com